W9-COZ-377

BLOOD CUT

Blood Cut was all about bad blood—the bad blood flowing through the veins of Roark Shado and the men he hired to do his fighting for him. Charging a five-dollar toll to cross the Blood River, Shado had dreams of turning his ugly little kingdom of prostitution and thievery into an empire.

Then three hard men crossed into Blood Cut—without paying a dime. A day ago they were strangers: Sam Diggs, a quiet, methodical detective; Isham Rye, a tall Texan driven on by the death of a woman; and Julius McCrea, who had ridden up from Fort Worth. The next morning the three war-scarred riders stood side by side in Blood Cut—each with their own motives and each ready both to fight and to die in a war against Roark Shado.

BLOOD CUT

Jack Curtis

This hardback edition 2003
by BBC Audiobooks Ltd
by arrangement with
Golden West Literary Agency

ISBN 0 7540 8250 4

British Library Cataloguing in Publication Data available.

Printed and bound in Great Britain by
Antony Rowe Ltd., Chippenham, Wiltshire

BLOOD CUT

1

Truly not named for any exceptional quantity of bloodshed in it or even nearby, the river was named for the Blood Indians, a tribelet of the Sioux, because it ran through their recently vacated hunting grounds.

They left not a single monument, edifice, or dwelling to mark a thousand years of living there. They left it as clean as they'd found it, and when they were gone it was as if they'd never been there except for the legacy of their name, which was accepted by the conquering Westerners.

A deep and devious river running roughly north and south, its banks were usually too high to make a fording, so that the few old, time-worn buffalo crossings became natural routes for western-bound immigrants.

Centered in a long bend of the river in upper Nebraska, the high banks of the river had been beaten down on either side by generations of buffalo to make a cut of natural sloping ramps into and out of the river. It was almost the only naturally safe crossing for a hundred miles either way, and it was known as Blood Cut.

The town lay on the west side of the bend, the land on the east being more exposed to the constant north wind and in wet years too boggy to trust.

On the east bank a signboard, crudely lettered, read: TOLL CHARGE $5.00 a wagon.

Nearby, where the flowing water was clear as a windowpane, Sam Diggs decided to make camp even though he could see the town over yonder, and he guessed the two-story building was a hotel with a water boiler, and next to it would be a saloon and dance hall with all the comforts of home.

Some said Sam Diggs was a plodder, dull and methodical. He preferred to think he was persistent as a bloodhound once he'd got a sniff of a crooked track. And if he ever thought about it, he supposed he was as good a looker as any other, never noticing in the mirror his long wedge of a nose and the weathered-down cheeks that made his eyes look so mournful even if he was feeling frisky as a spring yearling. He naturally stooped a bit because he was overtall, particularly with his boots and Stetson, and most doorways scared him.

He traveled alone.

Hauling the saddle and short rifle off his big bay and the pack off his pinto, he led the horses to the river to drink, then let them roll in a dry wallow.

Nothing dumber-looking than a horse lying belly-up with his legs crooked, wiggling around like he was trying to dig a grave for himself, Sam thought, waiting patiently.

When the bay and pinto had ground the itch out Sam led the horses over to a patch of deep grass and slipped on the rawhide hobbles.

Hauling a chunk of a log and a few branches from

the riverbank, he set up his kindling in a ring of fire-burned rocks already there.

It wasn't yet sundown, and he had plenty of time to reconnoiter the area for stray rattlesnakes or rabid skunks. He found only the grassy prairie, the crumbling riverbank, a nearly invisible lark's nest tucked into the high grass carrying two spotted eggs while the larks themselves pretended to stumble about trying to draw him away.

"Go easy, you two," he spoke aloud. "No need draggin' wings or gettin' all upset, because it's just me, and I don't aim to hurt a bird smaller'n a duck at least."

Smiling his mournful grimace, he paused, pivoted slightly on his left foot, crooked his shoulder, then stabbed his right hand to the walnut butt of his Colt .45. He drew, thumbed back the grooved hammer just as the big revolver came up level, and aimed at the yellow-breasted bird.

He had the morose feeling that he was slowing down.

"Sing, durn ya," he muttered, releasing the hammer and replacing the .45 in its holster as the birds scattered roundabouty to their nest.

From the town across the river he heard a pair of muffled shots.

They start early in Blood Cut, he thought, and he returned to camp. Digging in his saddle bags, he knew he'd only find the end of a slab of bacon, and he regarded it with distaste, knowing that over yonder he could set down in a restaurant and get a steak as big as a wagon wheel with a platter of potatoes and gravy, bakery bread, and plenty of hot coffee.

But he wasn't ready. One step at a time *Poco a poco.* You build your case slow and sure, and that way you don't go off on any false dodges. Maybe his man was over there, maybe he wasn't, but he sure as hell didn't want to scare him away after coming this far.

He thought it over again and decided his stomach could wait until morning before packing in a batch of flapjacks, steak and eggs, a couple pieces of apple pie, and a bottle of beer.

You're gettin' rattlebrained, he told himself, and then he thought that if you couldn't tease yourself some in this wide-open, lonely country with that sad wind singing its grief all day, you'd sure end up locoed.

He heard the rider coming from upriver before he cleared the cottonwoods at the bend. A big man on a big claybank. Texas double-rigged saddle. Carbine under his leg. Lasso by the horn and bedroll behind the high cantle. Sat himself in the stirrups like a cocked pistol. An impatient man with savvy enough to survive alone.

The rider checked the horse, studied the signboard, made up his mind, and put him in a fast walk toward Sam Diggs's camp.

Sam figured the rider would prefer to gallop, but it wouldn't be good manners to come in hard and fast on a stranger. So you come slow and let the stranger size you up. Give him time to ask you to light down and spread your blanket.

Sam Diggs did the sizing up and decided the tall rider with the big bulldogging shoulders was somebody to reckon with, but the pleasant blue eyes, broken nose, and straight-across mouth with grooves to either side all said the man was straight and could laugh at times, with no knavery, thievery, or backshooting. He was something, but not something for an honest man to fear.

"Howdy."

"Light and set awhile," Sam Diggs responded.

"Much obliged."

In those times you could give your right name, or you could give the wrong name or you could give nothing, and nobody would think much about it one way or the other, because it was a time for men to better themselves in the new land if they chose. In those days many a man with a cloud on his reputation changed his ways and died of old age as an honored pioneer, with no one ever knowing he'd altered his brand and rode the straight and narrow ever after.

"Name's Isham Rye," the stranger said flat out, humor sparkling in his blue eyes.

"I'm Sam Diggs. I been contemplating this here butt of a pork belly, considering whether to serve it with pecan pie or oyster stew."

Isham's smile let loose, and the grooves on his face deepened.

"Happens I've not got either one of them things, but I do have a fair-sized slab of corn pone a lady give me this mornin'."

"Isham Rye, you been sent by my stomach's guardian angel," Sam replied, his mournful expression never changing.

"Just let me put out this no-good, ungrateful hammerhead, and I'll be right with you." Isham led his horse down to the river to drink.

While Isham was caring for his horse Sam lighted the fire and dug out a frying pan from his saddlebags.

He was pleased. He hadn't talked much to anyone for a week, and though he was a reticent man, he liked company other than the mournful prairie wind.

And Isham Rye looked like a man worth talking to. Wasn't pushy. Wasn't sly. Wasn't foolish. What he was, maybe you'd never know for sure, but what he wasn't was easy to see.

Isham stacked his saddle and gear on the opposite side of the fire from Sam and found himself a spot out of the smoke.

"I come up from Abilene."

"Me, I'm from St. Joe."

"I figure to cross the river tomorrow and get a haircut and a drink."

"Staying on?" Sam asked diffidently. Folks hardly ever asked straight questions of strangers.

"You're an odd one," Isham chuckled, uncaring. "To tell the truth, I don't know whether I stay on here or not."

"Me, too." Sam made up for his prying. "I go day by day."

"You see the sign sayin' wagons have to pay to cross the river?"

"I seen it, but it don't sound right," Sam said. "If it was a ferry, it'd be different."

"And nobody owns the river," Isham added.

"I hear they got some fellers might shoot a man for not payin'," Sam said, covertly eyeing the worn Navy Colt .44 on Isham's hip.

"Sounds downright unfriendly." Isham smiled and dug into his saddlebag for a flat loaf of cornbread wrapped in newspaper.

From downriver Sam caught sight of a light spring wagon drawn by a pair of Spanish mules coming toward the ford. A bareback saddle horse trailed behind on a lead rope.

"Company," he said.

Isham turned to watch the driver stop and read the sign, pause to think it over, glance up their way at the fire, then turn the mules toward the camp.

"He ain't afraid anyways," Isham Rye said.

"I reckon he likes our price better."

The driver stopped his team and stepped down from the wagon before disturbing the camp.

A heavyset older man wearing a white panama straw hat, he stopped a few feet away and said, "I don't like that sign."

Sam regarded the older man. Dark skin, stocky and overweight, wearing undistinguished clothes except for beautifully tooled handmade boots and a linen duster, he stood straight up and down, his back like a ramrod.

"My name is Julius McCrea, and I come up from Fort Worth."

"Put up your mules and make yourself to home, Julius." Sam smiled his best old hound dog smile.

"Thanks. Can I offer a pot of beans and a few apples for supper?"

"You're the right man in the right place." Isham chuckled. "Looks like we're three of a kind."

As Julius McCrea unhooked the mules and the spare horse from the light wagon and led them to the river, Isham looked at Sam across the fire and said, "That makes three of us don't like crossing this river."

"Likely there's gunfighters hanging around Kansas cowtowns and down in the Nations would just be tickled pink to ride up this way and shoot anybody chargin' 'em for crossin', but I am not one of them."

"Me neither," Isham said, "but I reckon them fellers on the other side of the river is the same kind you're talkin' about, except they're already here settin' in the saddle."

"I guess we'll find out tomorrow," Julius said, coming to the fire from the gathering dusk.

"It's a hell of a long ride to get around it," Sam said.

"I don't want to ride around the cut. I want to go right on over there and see what makes 'em so special." Isham smiled.

"I've heard some bad things about those people that run Blood Cut."

"Then why come all the way from Fort Worth to meet up with them?" Sam asked bluntly.

"Simple business," Julius said carefully, putting his iron pot of beans on the fire next to the skillet.

After a long silence Isham ventured, "Must be quite a business."

"I thought you'd never ask." Julius chuckled. "Yes, it keeps me in beans. The fact is, if I sold guns and ammunition, where would be a better place to start than here?"

Sam glanced away. It didn't ring right. It didn't make him nervous or ornery, it just made a problem for him because he thought the chunky Texan was evading the truth.

What difference? People had a right to lie to strangers. Maybe the old Texan had a sack of gold in the wagon. Maybe he had a couple daughters hidden under the tarp. Whatever it was, it wasn't right, but then if it came his turn to talk about himself, he'd lie, too, and Isham, too, probably. Anybody knows you don't show your hole card first off.

Isham Rye knew Julius was lying, but it didn't rankle him enough to make him think twice. He considered asking him a tricky question about how many rounds a Remington .45-70 carried in its magazine, but why bother to prove what you already know?

"And you gentlemen are on the trail west?" Julius asked easily.

"I'm lookin' to locate a little ranch where I can bring my sick brother," Isham said. "This looks like pretty healthy country."

"A wonderful idea." Julius stirred the beans. "And you, Sam, are you, too, looking for a ranch?"

"I could say I'm prospectin' for gold"—Sam made his sorrowful smile—"but it's the dangdest coincidence. I also want to buy a little ranch where I can raise a family out of harm's way."

"You are both admirable men with unselfish ambitions," Julius said. "I'm proud to be admitted to your company."

"When them beans are hot, everything else is ready," Sam said, setting the skillet off the fire.

"Then let's eat. My stomach thinks my throat's been cut," Isham said.

"I'm sorry I forgot the champagne." Julius smiled.

"I heard a feller opened a bottle of champagne down in Abilene, and when the cork popped, four gunfighters killed him dead before the cork hit the ceiling," Isham said.

"Shoot first and ask questions later," Sam said, helping himself to the bean pot.

"Oh, now you're making a joke on me." Julius laughed, his ample midriff shaking.

"Well, I wasn't exactly there at the time," Isham said, smiling.

Julius McCrea, older and perhaps wiser, had his own doubts about his campmates. It hadn't been so easy leaving Fort Worth, what with Wes Hardin drinkin' and pawin' the ground like a bull in fly time, and John Selman and Clay Allison drinkin' and eyein' each other sidewise every night. Then the Mexicans gettin' fired up on mescal so raw it made even the worm brave, wantin' their land back, their cattle back, their women back, so between one faction and the other it wasn't easy to stay alive and well.

The pair of Army Colts he wore unobtrusively under the linen duster suited a man of his age and bearing, as well as giving him confidence enough to mingle with men carrying weapons of equal stopping power.

But at the moment, behind his good-natured smile, merry blue eyes, and chubby features, his mind was assessing his new acquaintances, trying to discard the chaff and shake out the real grain. They were clever, making it all the more difficult, but he read the silent signs in the depths of their eyes, in the things left unsaid, in the simplest gestures and easy humor, added them up and decided that on balance they were honest, definitely competent, and ready for bear.

"Best wash up before it gets too dark," Sam Diggs murmured, and, carrying his utensils, he walked down to the river edge with the others coming along after.

Squatting on the bank, scrubbing their plates, they listened to the river currents swirling by, frogs croaking, a muskrat splashing into his den, and then from upriver, on the opposite bank, they heard low voices, a heavy splash, and high, raucous laughter.

"Reckon I'll fetch my lass rope." Isham hurried off while the others neither spoke nor moved but kept their eyes on the river.

Slowly floating on the current, moving toward midstream, came an odd bundle barely discernible on the dark waters.

Coming closer, they saw a hand rise from the water and fall.

"I can't swim," Sam said, working to get his tight boots off.

"I can a little." Julius quickly shucked his gun belt, hat, short boots, and duster and charged into the water.

In a moment he was floundering in water over his head, still carried forward by the momentum of his first rush. After a moment his head came up, and he swam strongly if inexpertly toward midstream.

This time of the year the current of the Blood ran slow, giving Julius time enough to grab an arm. He had a brief glimpse of a young face. Turning the limp body over so that he could get his left arm around the chest, he lifted the white face from the water, then tried to swim back to shore with his right arm and a scissors kick.

He went under, swallowed water, and came up

sputtering and coughing, losing his bearings, then going under again.

Holding down the instinctive panic that wanted to override his thinking, he came up again, still gripping the youth, and forced himself to swim two strokes toward the bank before he started sinking again.

Desperately he raised the youth high and was sinking when he felt a lashing across his face, and the burden of the young man became buoyant, became light and airy—began moving, in fact, apparently of its own volition, toward the bank.

Instead of him carrying the load, the load was suddenly carrying him, and he clung to his former burden for dear life.

Coming up for air, he saw the rope that had caught the young man around the upper shoulders was stretched tight, and the current was arcing them toward shore. He tried to touch bottom with his feet, and the second time he found it, but he didn't release his hold on the youth because he suddenly found himself very, very tired.

A few seconds later he lay on the bank while nearby Isham worked over the back of the young man, pushing the water out and letting the good air come in.

He heard a groan, a coughing, and as he climbed to his feet Julius heard the young man yell, "Let me go!"

"Easy, son," Isham replied in a tone that would gentle a wild horse. "Easy now, you're safe now. So, now, so boss, easy does it."

"You swim pretty good," Sam said to Julius.

"Downstream I swim pretty good because I'm fat," Julius chuckled. "It's upstream that gives me a problem. I'm glad Isham is a master of the lasso."

"I'da liked to have tossed a figure eight on the both of you." Isham smiled. "Wouldn't that a been pretty?"

Before Julius could answer, the young man with the

blond curls climbed woozily to his feet and looked at his saviors in the dim light.

"Is this another cowboy game?" he asked, his voice high with anger and confusion.

"Steady down, son. We just done fished you out of the river. The rest of the story is yours to figure out," Sam said.

"I don't remember much. I was talking to Nan, and I heard something, and just as I turned somebody hit me." He fingered a lump on his head.

The young man's manner of speaking was different from the others' border drawls. It seemed too brittle and precise, like decorated tile alongside a common red brick.

"Yankee," Isham said.

"Philadelphia," the youth said. "My name's Anthony Burlington Barr, and someone attempted to kill me. Why?"

2

For Blood Cut, the night was just begun. Satisfied that there would be no more travelers coming across the river before morning, the three guards, with one idea, mounted their horses and rode from the river's edge to the Bucket Saloon some one hundred yards down the main street.

Their leader by default was a massive man known to have quick hands either for drawing his revolvers or for chopping a man's face to pieces with sharp left and right hooks. Under his stained, rumpled Stetson his greasy hair flowed straight down to his shoulders; his face, forever red and swollen like an angry viper's, was marked by a puckered black smear of gunpowder embedded in his right cheek. For that they called him Patch.

His companions, Mason and Virgil, both gaunt, wolfy men, wore their .45s tied low to the thigh with the holster trimmed to disencumber the draw. What distinguished them from each other was their teeth. Virgil had none, which made his grin a babylike, lippy horror, and Mason had many protruding buck teeth stained the color of tobacco ambeer.

Nearest the river stood the open-sided blacksmith shop made of poles and planks. The 140-pound anvil was fixed to a stump with railroad spikes, and the crude forge was a built-up mound of rocks and clay to which air was pumped from a primitive bellows made of two wide boards and a pliable antelope hide.

Next to the blacksmith was another shop that bore a sign saying Wagon Wheels Repaired. Next to that, of better construction, was a harness shop, which had a steel spring bow of brass bells over the doorway. Here the boardwalk started as the town attained the plain level.

Adjacent was the Niobrara Café, which was a large room encompassing a big Spark cast-iron stove with shiny nickeled decorations, cupboards, plank tables, and assorted chairs and benches. The dishes were washed in a tin tub out in the back alley.

Next was the freshly painted two-story Dew Drop Inn hotel, with eight rooms to rent.

The Mercantile was easily the biggest building in town because it contained most everything a person needed, from fresh beef to blasting powder, bolts of calico to alcohol-fortified patent medicines for those good women who weren't allowed to drink in the Bucket Saloon.

On the corner stood the Bucket Saloon, the only other two-story building in town.

On the opposite side of the block were the Drover's Bank, McDowell's Furniture and Mortuary, the barber and cobbler shops, both run by Mr. André Brown, and next to that, its boundaries stretching to the river, the livery stable and corrals.

Beyond that, one block to the west, was a hodgepodge of hide dealers, wood yards, feed and grain and farm supply outfits that dwindled off into mud-chinked, picket-post shacks.

Laid out behind either side of Main Street were a few clapboard houses built or being built for the people who lived there.

Someone had tried to plant alfalfa in Main Street to hold down the dust, but it only grew in protected little coverts where perhaps a swamper dumped a bucket of sudsy water once in a while.

So it was at the end of the block on the north side that Patch, Virgil, and Mason dismounted, tied their horses with the others at the rail, and strode into the Bucket Saloon.

Not without reason did Patch pause at the batwing doors and survey the inside of the saloon. Man could get hisself kilt bumping into a hombre on the prod, he thought. Besides, it don't hurt to know who you were going to meet inside.

Looked easy enough. A couple shady-looking cow-hands who worked at odd times for Rainy Day, a baldheaded drummer in a suit, four poker players at the round green baize table. A couple sporting girls in skimpy outfits at the end of the bar waiting for André Brown to come over and play the accordion.

At the other table in the corner Patch made out the four men who counted most in the town of Blood Cut.

Without seeing his hairless, pale face, Patch recognized Rainy Day by the ivory grips on the .45s that nestled in polished black tooled-leather holsters. A tiny shiver ran down his backbone when he saw that slim back, the beautiful guns, one hand apparently resting on his right leg, except Patch knew that hand never rested, that hand seemed to have a life of its own. One little whisper of dissent or danger and that hand would fill with a Colt in less than one second, and someone would be dead with a head shot. There was no getting around it, Rainy Day was the flat out best, and Patch wanted nothing to do with him.

"There's Rainy," he said softly.

"You'd think this town could support two saloons," Virgil grumbled, knowing he couldn't enjoy himself in the same room with the man in black.

"Why don't you give him a ball to the back of his head?" Mason whispered through his yellow teeth.

"Go ahead," Patch said, seeing a second man in the shadows.

Everett Potter, benign, steel-rimmed spectacles glittering, dressed in a hard-weave suit, banker written all over him.

Opposite Everett Potter sat the marshal in a cowhide vest, his belly doubling over his cartridge belt. He called himself Bud Stebbins, but he could just as well have called himself Joe Human for all anyone cared.

In the group was a once-handsome woman of indeterminate years with an upswept and hennaed wig like a torch, and a crimson face so covered with makeup only her reptilian eyes and hard slash of a mouth stood out. She smoked a thin cigar and idly tapped the table with fat fingers marred by greenish-gold rings. She called herself Lily.

Facing the group and speaking with slow emphasis was Roark Shado, the southern gentleman. Immaculate in every way, Roark Shado was a picture of sartorial splendor in this frontier town. He wore a soft cream-colored felt hat, a dark frock coat, a pleated and starched white shirt, and a silk cravat with a diamond stickpin that sparkled like the sun even in the lamplight. His narrow face bore a fine flowing brown mustache. Through deep-set eyes under overhanging brows he watched like a raptorial bird, every inch an aristocrat and definitely not a dude. Those soft, long fingers could stroke out any card they wanted from a fresh deck. They could make dice eat from his hand, and they could produce from the sleeve, the vest, the placket, the boot, the hat (or even thin air if pushed hard enough) a .36-caliber Navy Colt which was, after all, about all anyone needed for self-defense.

Patch had seen both Roark Shado and Rainy Day in action at different times, and he knew that gentleman Roark Shado was the fastest, toughest, and smartest.

"I just want one drink," Patch said, angry at himself for being put off by men hardly more dangerous than himself. Especially in the right time and place, he could beat any of them.

He could have it all if things went right. The cheroots, the brandy, the clothes, the guns, the girls. Could have anything he wanted if he waited.

In Patch's mind there were no rules in gunfighting. If you could manage to shoot your man in the back with a long-range rifle from ambush, so much the better.

Patch led his underlings, one on either side, toward the far end of the bar where the harmless drummer sipped at a glass of red whiskey thinned with Blood River water.

"What'll it be, gents?"

"Three glasses and the bottle," Patch said angrily, because the bartender knew all along what they wanted and didn't need to waste time talking.

One of these days I'll just put a ball right up his big nose, he thought, and he slopped whiskey into the three greasy glasses.

Everyone else all dressed up and been to the barber shop, he thought, but not the boys collecting the toll and taking all the abuse. No, they just get a bad time from a tinhorn bartender and cheap liquor. Damn it!

"Here's to better days," Patch growled, lifting his glass.

"I'll drink to that." Virgil grinned, his pink gums protruding over his lips.

"I'm in." Mason tossed down the clear, holding his breath as it scalded his throat.

"We did pretty good today," Virgil said, wiping his rubbery mouth with the back of his hand. "Two wagon trains. Five dollars a wagon. It adds up."

"Sure," Patch muttered, "but then Johnny-on-the-spot here comes Rainy with his hand out before we can even pocket a red cent. I don't call that so good."

"What the hell," Mason said, "we're doin' better'n some thirty-dollar-a-month cowhand out riding lonesome day and night."

"I just wonder if Rainy handed all that money over to the boss." Virgil rolled his eyes sideways.

"It don't pay to wonder what goes on over there," Patch said, and he poured again, thinking how he'd buffaloed both the wagonmasters with him in front and Virgil and Mason sneaking around behind them. A hundred and ten dollars from the first one and eighty-five from the second.

"You pay here, or you go back where you come from, I don't care."

No, they didn't like it. Always playing poor-mouth. Women and children. Need to buy supplies. Babies to feed. No money. Hard winter. Swap you a couple weaner pigs . . . The women and girls all hiding back in the wagons, knowing well enough what was in his mind was they to trouble him overmuch. So they had to give over the money and go on through town without stopping, and about the time a man begins to feel he's being paid a fair wage, here comes Rainy Day with his hand out and his eyes hard as diamonds.

It don't seem right, he thought. After all, we did the work. We took the chances. We even picked up the girl, and not a cent for that either. No, it ain't hardly right.

The punchers were nursing their drinks, aware of the tension. They'd been just a pair of broke cowboys trying to get back to Texas after thinking they could retire in Montana, only to find out they had to do footwork at a ranch, like fencing and cutting hay for less money than they could make settin' a horse in Texas. They'd managed to buy new jeans and shirts in Miles City, but they'd spent their money before they got to buy new boots and hats. So they'd drifted south and met Rainy Day, who had sized them up and hired them. They had gathered the cattle with no questions asked, but payday was still two weeks off.

Still, a young man always hopes against hope he's a miracle of manhood, and the two loose-ended, slightly illegal cowboys were no different. They occasionally cast a longing eye at the two bar ladies, both overweight and sulky in their garments of feathers and pink gauze, who knew their type and played by the rule: You get what you pay for first. Maybe you get something you didn't pay for, too, but you charge that up to experience.

Lily left the table and walked up a stairway to the second floor, which appeared to be dark and empty.

André Brown came through the batwing doors with his accordion and his kitty jar, playing a few lively chords with his right hand. A roundy, roly-poly, jolly-faced cherub with a short beard, he came to the bar, where the bardog had already poured him a glass of the clear. In a second he tossed it off, put the kitty jar on the bar, and faced the two sporting girls.

"What would you like to hear, Lorena?"

"'The Girl I Left Behind Me.'"

"No, a polka. Something lively!" the other said.

Swinging into a polka, André Brown did a few lively kick steps himself before settling down to play the tune. The women held hands and danced in place while the poor cowboys watched longingly.

Even Patch's humor improved with the music, and he was wondering if the younger of the pair would take his IOU when the cheery scene was broken by a scream and an oath, then the sound of a door slamming. Everyone in the room, including those at the table of Roark Shado, turned to the upstairs balcony, where a girl who looked to be no more than seventeen years of age rushed into the light.

Her hair was soft and golden and flowed in curls to her shoulders. Her face was milk white and spotted with freckles, and her flashing green eyes looked downstairs a moment as if hoping for safety. Seeing no friends there, she turned to face her attacker, who came from a dark hall. Lily, the dark-faced, barrel-shaped woman with the red wig, came forward slowly, a braided rawhide quirt in her right hand.

"Get back in here."

"I will not. I want loose!" the girl responded, staring into the hypnotic eyes of the older woman.

"Get back in there, I say!"

"I will not!" the girl cried out, backing up against the railing, thereby revealing a bleeding welt on her back.

"What's goin' on?" the tallest cowboy asked into the silence.

"Better you get back to your mavericks," Patch said, sizing up the cowboy.

"You mean you allow whippin' of women?" the cowboy retorted angrily.

"I mean if you work for Blood Cut, you keep shut." Patch had already vaguely decided to kill the cowboy just to make himself feel better after having such a bad day. Still, it all had to be played out to look fair and square.

As if to emphasize the point, the blocky woman cracked the quirt across the girl's face, making her cry out.

"Watch my back, John," the cowboy said. "I'm goin' on up there."

"Stay where you are, cowboy," Patch snarled.

The cowboy stared at Patch in disbelief. The room was silent, as if waiting for the arrival of Death on a pale white horse.

Roark Shado grinned at Rainy Day and winked. Day nodded.

"Just a moment, please." Shado rose and faced the room, his soft voice carrying something more than sorghum and hambone intonation—carrying the intangible tone of command, an indefinable power of voice and manner that asserted itself by itself. It wasn't from the hideout derringer near his fingertips, it was in the straightness of his back and the probing, deep-set eyes.

His gaze roved the room, fixing each person in place, then came back to the man sitting opposite him.

"Mr. Day, I understand this establishment is your business, but I mean to stop the whipping of that girl."

"Go ahead, Shado." Rainy Day spoke slowly, as if fetching up his speech from memory. "I run the saloon, Lily runs the dry stock. It ain't no affair of mine."

"Marshal, it behooves you to keep the peace while I go up those stairs. That suit you, Mr. Day?"

Rainy Day stared at the tall southerner, started to speak, changed his mind, and shrugged his shoulders.

The potbellied marshal with debauched, cloudy features rose slowly, gun in hand, to face Patch and the drifters.

"You all settle down or I'll do it for you."

Roark Shado moved swiftly up the stairs. Putting himself between the blond girl and the blocky brute of a woman named Lily, he said, "No more of this."

"She works for me," the woman said stubbornly.

"That's not true," the blond girl said. "They said my daddy was up here and needed me. It's all lies."

"What's your name, my dear?"

"Nan Packard. Daddy's name is Walter. Our ranch is just a ways north of here."

"May I take you home, Miss Packard?"

"I'd be ever so much obliged," Nan Packard said with a warm smile of relief.

3

I been wanting to meet you for some weeks now, Tony," Sam Diggs said across the fire to the young man.

"Me?" Anthony Burlington Barr asked with surprise. "Why?"

"Your daddy's assistant vice president back east, he wrote and asked me to see you got back home safe," Sam said.

"Why you?"

"It's my line of work, doing things nobody else will do. I keep an office in St. Joe, but I travel about, independent like."

"You mean you're a private detective, like a Pinkerton?"

"I suppose that's close enough."

"How much is he paying you to bring me back?" Tony's voice rose to a higher, more strained note.

"I'd rather not say."

"Is it like a bounty, where you bring me home dead or alive?" The young man's face was flushed, his eyes wild as he remembered the stern, unyielding father who had so constricted his life that he'd fled in rebellious desperation.

"Easy now, lad," Julius said mildly. "Sometimes fathers seem like they're hard-boiled tyrants, but most of the time they're only tryin' to guide their children the best way they know how."

"Guide?" the blond youth exclaimed. "That's a joke! He had my job picked out for me, my wife, my home, my club, and probably my place in heaven, too. No, thanks, Mr. Sam Diggs, I'll just live my own life, if you don't mind."

"I don't much mind you livin' your own life, son" —Sam Diggs smiled his hound-dog grimace—"it's just I'm hired to bring you back there and talk to him. That's what I aim to do. After that, you're clear."

"You can't . . . you wouldn't force me . . . "

"I hope it don't come to that."

Young Anthony Barr looked at Julius and Isham for help or at least confirmation of his worst fears, but they stared stolidly at the fire, minding their own business.

"Look, Mr. Diggs—"

"Call me Sam. We're goin' to be travelin' together."

"Look, Sam, there's a girl here somewhere. I've got to find her."

"Why?"

"Why? Well, to tell the truth—I want to marry her."

"I don't think you better get married until later," Sam said with certainty. "I think maybe your daddy has that on his mind."

"You see, he won't even let me pick out my own wife."

"If you don't mind my sayin' so," Julius murmured apologetically, "you're a bit young for marriage, aren't you?"

"I'm eighteen, and I've been living on my own for the past three months." Tony tried to be persuasive.

"Still, there are lots of ladies to look at before you get yourself hogtied," Sam said. "Ain't that right, Isham?"

"I never tried it." The big cowboy smiled. "You, Sam?"

"I did try it. That's why I moved to St. Joe and changed my name." Sam chuckled.

"What happened to her?" Tony asked, suddenly interested.

"Likely she's back home with her mama, and both of them are noddin' at each other, clucking away about all the bad things men do."

"You just up and left?" Tony asked, admiration creeping into his voice.

"It was either that or shoot her." Sam's eyes were twinkling with humor. "And she wasn't worth the powder."

"Do you have a family, Julius?" Tony asked, seeking an ally.

"I have seven children, all girls. They are all living at the home place just outside Fort Worth."

"You see?" Tony exclaimed to Sam. "If Julius can do it, I can do it."

"How long you been married, Julius?" Sam asked.

"Married?" Julius's eyes widened with fun. "Who said anything about marriage? I'm never home long enough to get married!"

"You're only making fun of me. Nobody ever takes me seriously," Tony complained.

"You're still learnin', son," Isham said, not unkindly.

"I guess I'll just have to do it my own way, even if I owe you my life."

"Before you get yourself all fashed up," Sam said,

"mind tellin' us how you found yourself takin' a bath in the river with your clothes on?"

"I was out north where Nan lives, trying to see her—"

"You mean she don't want to see you?" Sam asked.

"Well, she thinks I'm just an obnoxious greenhorn, you know, and I haven't had time to prove otherwise yet." Tony flushed.

"Go on with your story," Julius said.

"She was going out riding, and I figured to meet her at the river, but three riders caught up with her first. Time I got there, they'd told her that her father was sick and needed her. I told her to hold off and go on with me, and about then the one that had no teeth hit me over the head with his six-shooter, and that's all I remember. I've got to find her before it's too late."

"Wait a second, Tony," Sam said, feeling aggravated.

He was tired. Worse, he was beginning to worry about old age creeping up on him. He'd been on the go for six weeks looking for this boy, and he wanted a night's sleep. Now the kid wanted to go tree the whole territory looking for a girl that didn't want him around.

"There's no time to wait! Those three toughs were not proper company for her."

"Where did they go?"

"They said they were going to Blood Cut, that her father was there waiting. I'm going right now!" Tony leapt to his feet, ready to charge across the river, when he realized he had no horse, no weapon, not even a hat.

"Would you mind lending me a horse and coming along with me?" he asked Sam, shamefaced.

"I can't think of anything more enjoyable," Sam said, "except maybe just snuggling up to my saddle and having a good night's sleep."

"Please," Tony begged. "She may be in danger."

Sam shook his head with exasperation. "All right, let's go."

"Need any help?" Julius asked.

"No, thanks, I don't aim to barge in there with guns a-blazin'. We're just goin' to have a look-see so my young companion can go back to Philadelphia with an easy mind."

Saddling up Sam's horses, the veteran detective and the youth rode off toward the ford. Splashing across the river, they saw the empty toll booth next to the livery stable and proceeded into town.

A lamp burned in the jail, but most of the street was dark.

"Any place certain she'd go?"

"I didn't hear, but there's a man name of Rainy runs the town. I think he owns the saloon."

"That wouldn't be Rainy Day, would it?" Sam asked.

"That sounds right. Do you know him?"

"By reputation only. I wish I was goin' the other way."

As they passed the jail Sam saw a portly man wearing a badge come out and stop to lock the door.

"Evenin', Marshal," Sam offered.

"Evenin'." The marshal turned toward them. "What can I do for you?"

"We're lookin' for a yellow-headed girl name of Nan—"

"You're too late."

"She been here?"

"She was here, but Roark Shado took her home in his buggy."

"Who's Roark Shado?" Tony demanded.

"Mind your manners, boy." The marshal's voice was cold. "I got a special place for troublemakers."

"Don't worry, Marshal, boys will be boys, y'know,"

Sam offered cheerfully, and he reined his horse over to the rail in front of the Bucket Saloon.

As they prepared to step inside Sam said gently, "Son, keep a dally on your tongue. You might learn more listenin' than talkin'."

Crossing the scarred plank floor to the bar, Sam Diggs swept the room with his eyes hidden under his hat brim. The two drifters had gone, replaced by the blacksmith and another townsman. The two bar girls were teasing the drummer as André Brown cavorted about, playing the accordion.

Banker Everett Potter, bawdy Lily, and Rainy Day occupied the far table, idly playing five-card stud.

Three hard cases stared at the kid.

"I'll have a whiskey. He don't want nothin'," Sam told the bartender.

Tony's face flushed angrily, but he kept quiet.

The sporting girls perked up when they saw Sam, patting the spit curls on their foreheads, adjusting their bodices for the best possible presentation, practicing come-hither looks.

"That's the three toughs that took Nan off," Tony whispered.

"I seen the bald gums before," Sam said sotto voce, nodding. "Maybe we can kinda slip out the way we come in."

At the other end of the bar Patch and his cronies broke off their stares, huddled, and spoke in voices too low to understand, but by their occasional glances at Tony and Sam the object of their confabulation was obvious.

Sam swallowed the whiskey and returned the empty glass to the bar.

"Fill it up again, bardog," Patch called to the bartender.

"No, thanks." Sam turned the glass over. "One is all the doctor ordered."

"One more for the road."

Virgil drifted off to the right of the group as if on a prearranged signal, his pale lips peeled away from his gums, his hand dangerously close to the butt of his Colt.

"Wait," Sam said, sidling a step to the left to be clear of the boy, "now let me tell you what I think before somebody gets it wrong."

"I reckon you think you're too good to drink with us." Virgil took control.

"I reckon it was you that hit this young man over the head this afternoon. Sticks in your craw he's still around, and you been elected clean-up man."

"You got a big mouth, mister." Virgil's cupped hand hovered over the walnut butt of the .45, his eyes fixed on Sam's hands.

"Virgil." Rainy's acid-sharp voice cut into the tension. "Virgil, that feller goes by the name of Sam Diggs."

"Means nothin' to me," Virgil gritted out.

"I'm just trying to save your life." Rainy Day grinned.

"I don't need jokin' right now." Virgil's voice was rising. "The son of a bitch won't drink with us. I want to see him draw—"

Keyed on to the word of insult, Sam drew and fired as Virgil's hand stabbed for his revolver. Sam's massive 128-grain lead ball smashed in Virgil's whole chest before going on through and taking out his spinal column. Virgil's own bullet ploughed a groove in the floor and sent splinters flying at the two women at the end of the bar.

Not waiting to see the devastation wrought by his bullet, Sam swung the Colt to the right, and Patch and Mason put their hands on the bar.

"You could have let him live another second and still killed him,' Rainy Day said judiciously.

"C'mon, boy," Sam said, "blood makes me giddy."

"You ever need work, Mr. Diggs, come see me," Rainy Day offered. "You can have Virgil's place and work on up."

"I've got my hands full right now, Mr. Day," Sam said without turning his eyes from Patch and Mason. "Maybe later on."

Tony went ahead of Sam out the door, and as Tony mounted, Sam kept his Colt aimed directly at the batwing doors, ready for a foolhardy rush.

"I wish I had a gun," Tony said.

"Thank heavens you don't," Sam said, mounting up. Turning the horse down the street toward the river, he kicked him into a hard gallop with Tony riding close by.

They sent spray flying as they crossed the Blood. Sam rode straight east for a mile, just in case someone was following, then led Tony in a wide circle back to their camp.

The fire had burned low. Julius had bedded down in the back of his wagon, and Isham Rye lay nearly hidden off in the shadows, his head cradled by his saddle.

Sam thought both of them were awake but wouldn't move a whisker unless he spoke up. He gave an extra blanket to Tony, then took time to clean the six-gun and reload.

Leading the way out of the light of the glowing embers, he found a flat place to bed down and figured Tony could do the same. If he couldn't, then he'd no doubt learn.

Watching the brilliant crystal stars wheel slowly over the prairie land, he tried to settle himself down. He hadn't wanted to kill the man called Virgil; it was the other way around. Virgil probably thought he was an old, worn-out drover, or maybe he thought he was a retired goat herder, and even after Rainy

Day had warned him he had still kept on his fatal course.

I was slow, he thought, too slow.

It was always the way. Some hot-handed gunfighter taking a look at the slow-drawling hound dog, looking like an easy mark, a granger, a bumpkin, not understanding that the jowly, sad-eyed hombre had lived thirty years on the frontier, and it took more than luck to do that.

Rainy knew it. He hadn't wanted a fight. Another survivor, he knew enough to stay sober most of the time, to keep his guns clean and loaded and his tracks covered.

Thinking about Rainy, he wondered why the black-clad gunfighter was so far off his range. Most times he liked the border country down Texas way. Sometimes he rode over into Mexico if he heard of easy plunder, other times he was known to ride to the railroad towns where the banks were full of new northern money. He only needed one good haul every six months or a year, because he wasn't that bad of a poker player.

It was said, too, that he had no compunction about killing for money. For a thousand dollars he'd pick a fight with a Pinkerton, or a governor, or another gunslinger, and collect.

Why would such a top-money gun be wasting his time in the little town of Blood Cut? Why had he hired Patch, Mason, and Virgil? What was there to steal?

The crossing had the potential to be extremely valuable if he could make his toll gates stick, but he had already done that. What else was there?

Have to watch the boy, Sam thought. He'd be looking for a chance to run free. Didn't blame him much, but his job was already settled, the contract signed. And if word got around you were getting too old to cut the mustard, you'd be spending your time counting flyspecks on the calendar.

Tony didn't have to marry anyone. It wasn't that serious, but his father did intend for him to take over the business sometime.

Only natural, he decided. Been going on ever since dynasties started. You build up until it falls down. Sometimes it never falls down. Would the Astors and the Vanderbilts ever have to work for their bread again? No. Probably not. Once you have so much money, there's no way to turn it off.

His own father had been a cotton merchant in Memphis, buying, selling, and shipping, and no doubt he wanted his son to take over the business and make it bigger. But the war stopped all that, and his father had died with nothing to bequeath to his son, and his son had emerged from the War Between the States with little hope.

At Antietam and afterward Sam had lost faith in God, money, property, ideas, and the world in general. All he wanted was to live and let live, but he couldn't even do that. It came down to the fact that the world was nothing except life and death, and the only gain was survival.

In truth, he hadn't ever married because the girl he left behind him had married another man, then become pregnant and a widow, in that order. She wasn't all that attractive by the time Sam came limping home.

At least, though, she'd cured him of thinking seriously about the opposite sex. He'd decided it didn't pay to think of them as anything but a joke that nature played on men. Thinking that way, he could keep his distance and his sense of humor, too.

Oh, they wiggle and they giggle
And they'll sit on your lap.
Oh, they'll titter and they'll twitter
Until they snap the trap.

Snap . . . snap . . . snap . . . Sam awakened suddenly, aware now that it was not a dream. It was the crackling of brush, and he leapt from his blanket looking for his hat and boots.

Thus attired, he saw first that the boy was gone, along with his blanket. Awkwardly running through the first pink tones of dawn, he found his big bay grazing peaceably, but the pinto was gone.

The kid had ridden off in a hurry, at the last second discarding or forgetting the blanket.

That kid, if nothing else, was worth a good deal of money as well as professional pride to Sam Diggs, and he had no intention of losing either one at this late date.

Leading the bay back to camp, he saddled him quickly and tied his saddlebags behind.

"In a hurry?" Isham asked, rising up from his blanket.

"Kid's gone with my pony."

"Don't worry about your gear," Julius said, coming from his wagon. "I'll either be here or in town. I hope you catch the boy before he gets into a hornet's nest."

"Be careful of that town. Seems like a gent name of Rainy Day runs it, and he's faster'n me." Sam smiled sadly and mounted the bay.

"I've got no business with him," Julius said.

"Me neither," Isham muttered, as if disappointed.

Sam whirled the bay and galloped north until he came into the woods along the river and had to slow to a walk.

Isham Rye built up the fire and started a pot of coffee.

"You know that Rainy Day feller?"

"I know of him. He comes from south Texas, but I never met him," Julius said carefully. "All I know is he's faced the best gunfighters, and he's still walking around," he added silently.

"That don't always count. Them kind of folks hardly ever fight fair, so it gets down to who is the dirtiest or sneakiest, not the fastest or the bravest."

"You have something there. Usually the king is sitting down, having a drink, talking to a girl, playing cards, and along comes a John Selman or a Jack McCall and just shoots his man in the back of the head. I know many cases like that, but it's a game I don't play."

"Me neither, Julius, not less I have to," Isham said softly.

"There is the matter of honor." Julius nodded. "Sometimes a man must go against good sense and bad odds because he cannot live with himself otherwise."

"I'm agreeable."

"Tell me, Isham, what do you really want?" Julius asked straight out. "Who are you looking for? Maybe I can help you."

"I'm huntin' a certain whoremaster. I figure he's over in Blood Crossing.

"You mean to kill him?"

"Well, now"—Isham grinned wolfishly, his eyes like bullets—"I don't mean to just kill him first off. First I want to skin him alive and whittle off a few choice parts of him. Then I figure to salt him down good before puttin' him on the fire."

4

Julius studied the broad-shouldered westerner across the fire. He'd gauged the man wrong the first time.

Rye could pass for a cowpuncher with his hat, flannel shirt, jeans, and battered dogger boots, but punchers didn't talk about roasting their enemies over a fire.

He wasn't an easterner. The pattern of his speech was deep southern, perhaps Louisiana born and raised, maybe went to war, maybe went west.

He wasn't a gunfighter, although he was probably as fast as any of them. Julius knew that type well enough. They didn't ride the trails much, preferring hotel beds and restaurant meals and saloon whiskey. They were nervous men, always trying to look calm. Hickok was nervous, Masterson was nervous, the Earps were nervous underneath their show of indolence.

Maybe he had a little ranch on down the trail, just getting started on the lonesome. What was going on behind those icy gray eyes? How could he joke about flaying a man and roasting him alive?

Julius leafed through the wanted posters in his

mind, but there wasn't a face even close to the prairie-tanned, rough-hewn countenance of Isham Rye.

Possibly he was a livestock inspector or an undercover operator for the Cattleman's Association, possibly even a bounty hunter talking big, making a smoke screen about himself. For sure, a bounty hunter wouldn't even think of destroying the man he wanted to bring in. Didn't make sense.

Not a Bible thumper either. No mercy in him, not by a long shot. About all you could pin down was that Isham Rye was a competent outdoorsman, and judging from the scars and bent nose, he never backed down.

Had some money. His saddle was a Harmon. His six-gun was the latest improved Colt, his hat Stetson, and Julius would have bet his mules that the boots were handmade by Luis Javier Fajardo in San Antonio. His soogan was a fringed, soft-tanned doeskin bag made extra large to fit his frame and folded up neat and tidy to mate the back of the saddle.

First-class rigging, but he didn't sport a gold ring or a silver belt buckle, not even a concha on his hatband.

Living on the border most of his life, mingling with all manner of men, high and low, rich and poor, Julius McCrea had learned to observe men the way an Indian learns to read tracks, and he was rarely wrong in his judgment, but Isham Rye had him stumped.

"You said you came up from Texas?" Julius asked casually.

"I don't think I said that exactly." Isham blew on his coffee.

"It's no crime if you did," Julius said dryly.

"Fact is, I come roundy-bouty from the west."

"California?"

"That's right." Isham nodded. "I just taken up a

little spread between San Juan Bautista and Salinas, half hills and half valley."

"You've come a long way just to smoke out a man."

"But not much farther to go."

Deciding it was futile to try to learn more about Isham and his mission, Julius stood away from the fire, rinsed out his blue enameled cup, and said, "We're getting nowhere setting around here."

"Hold on a bit. Someone's coming." Isham shifted his position, clearing his six-gun.

Julius looked back toward the prairie but saw nothing.

"From the south. Through the trees."

A group of five riders emerged from the timber, led by a lean bed-slat of a man with a walrus mustache. Isham noticed they were travel-stained and weary, although they rode their tired horses like a war party ready to attack. None of them had shaved in a week, and Isham guessed they hadn't eaten a square meal in a day and a half.

"You there!" the leader called. "Hold it right there."

"We wasn't asking permission to leave," Isham came right back at him.

"What are you doing here?" the head man demanded.

"What are you looking for?" Isham rejoined.

"Yes," Julius said, smiling, "what's your problem?"

"Search 'em, Ed," the head man said to the rider on his right.

At that moment the new Colt appeared in Isham's big hand and aimed directly at the heart of the boss.

"Nobody searches me while I'm alive," Isham said. "Now you get your thin butt outa my camp before I do something crazy, like the last time a burrhead bothered me."

The head man glanced at his crew.

"It don't make any difference what they do to me." Isham's eyes blazed like blue lightning. "It's what I'm goin' to do to you."

Staring at the barrel of the .45, the head man thought it was growing bigger and bigger, and pretty soon it looked like a railway tunnel ready to swallow him up.

"I'm backing up," he said carefully.

"What are you looking for?" Julius put in quickly, trying to change the direction of the conflict and reduce the tension.

"Six hundred beeves branded Block Diamond and the two men that rustled 'em."

"You looked north?"

"They ain't north and they ain't south. We been riding for a week. The trail ends back yonder in a scree of loose rock."

"We haven't seen 'em," Isham said, "but if they're not on this side of the river, likely they're on the other."

"I asked those gunsels taking toll, and I asked the marshal, and I asked in the saloon. Nobody saw them beeves use the crossing."

"Can't help you, then," Isham said. "Likely the Indians taken 'em north faster'n you figured."

"Wasn't Indians. These scalawags rode shod horses. And you can put that hogleg down now. I reckon I come on some salty at you."

"I reckon."

Isham settled the Colt back in its holster.

"Any ideas?"

"Just one. If they aren't east of the river, they're west, no matter what anybody told you."

"You mean they're all in cahoots?" The skinny rider closed his little bug eyes a moment, thinking hard on the notion.

"Where were you headed?" Julius asked.

"Miles City, but we ain't goin' to make it this way," the rider said quickly. He jerked his head, wheeled his horse, and led the way toward the crossing.

"That town is beginning to smell like it would draw flies," Isham muttered.

"You're fast as a cat with his tail afire," Julius said. "What would you have done if one of them had tried for a draw?"

"I figured you could handle the rest of 'em." Isham let a smile cross his lips.

"Thanks for your confidence, Isham, but next time don't count on so much from so little." Julius grinned.

"You crossin'?"

"Sure am."

Climbing up to the spring wagon seat, Julius waited until Isham had joined him on the big claybank, then clucked to the small mules and guided them toward the crossing.

He noticed that the ford was broad enough to trail twenty steers abreast, and their tracks would soon be covered up by riders with remudas, or other cattle and wagons.

Isham was certainly right: Either they crossed here or they didn't cross at all.

Yet the marshal and the bartender had denied seeing them. As a general rule marshals lied more than bartenders, in Julius's experience, but rarely would both of them lie together.

Unless they were all paid by the same man.

That man could be Rainy Day, because he had never worked for anyone in his whole life, probably because most bosses would be afraid to hire him.

They passed the toll shack, where Patch and Mason sat on a bench, hats low over their eyes.

"You there," Patch called to Isham, "that'll be fifty cents for you and your horse."

"No," Isham said.

"You hear me?" Patch yelled, getting to his feet.

"Damn it, I told you once, no!" Isham turned the horse to face the big gunman, plainly intending to fight him if there was another word of argument.

"Aw, what's fifty cents," Patch growled, sitting on the bench again. "Cheapskates."

He was too unnerved to question Julius or charge for the spring wagon. He had a throbbing headache and a sour stomach, his eyes were too bloodshot to see clearly, and his hands were trembling too much to shoot straight.

"Damn that rotten red whiskey," he groaned, holding his head in his hands. "I feel like I swallered a sick skunk."

"Likewise," Mason murmured.

"Shut the hell up!" Patch roared. "You talk too damn much."

Julius and Isham passed up the slope where the massive blacksmith in a leather apron was pounding cold iron and went on to the main street.

"Ready for some ham and eggs?" Julius asked.

Isham stood in his stirrups, surveying the street and building, hideouts and coverts, the marshal sitting on a bench in front of the jail, a man sweeping the boardwalk. Women dressed for shopping. Water troughs, false fronts, and open windows, all of it registered in his head, just in case.

They stopped in front of the Niobrara Café and went inside.

Three men and a woman sat at the table in the rear. One was dressed immaculately in black, one was dressed in a gray frock coat and flannel trousers, and the third wore a business suit. The older, painted woman wore a pink satin dress with ribbons and lace.

Julius promptly sat at an empty table near the door, nodding to Isham. He knew already he'd have a problem with his appetite, because that foursome gave off an electric shock that overcame hunger.

"You're too late for breakfast," a large, gray-haired lady called to them from the stove.

"We'll have dinner, then." Isham smiled.

"What'd you like?"

"Ham and eggs and about a foot and a half of flapjacks." Isham hoped she had some sense of humor.

Once she sorted it out, she laughed. "All right, have it your way. Two orders of ham and eggs and flappers comin' up."

In a moment she brought them mugs of coffee and mopped the plank table with a wet towel.

"You folks passin' through?"

"We're both looking for a place to settle down. Julius is more interested in town livin' than me."

"Well, we need all the good people we can get," she declared with a straight face, keeping her eyes away from the other table.

"Looks like a nice place for a man with a family," Julius said.

"Stop and stay awhile," she said as she went back to the great iron stove.

"I guess we could put up at the hotel for a few days," Isham said. "What do you think, Julius?"

"Fine with me. You can scout the back country for your ranch, and I can inquire around about business."

The men at the other table had quit talking and were listening to Isham and Julius, who were starting on their breakfast.

The paunchy man in the worsted suit rose and started for the door, and the tall man in the gray frock coat and trousers followed.

Isham noted that he wore well-made boots, but the yellow-dyed leather disturbed his sense of harmony. That color of yellow boots was something a kid might dream of wearing, but it wasn't right for a gentleman in a ruffled shirt. When he was younger they'd called that particular color calf-splatter, and though as a boy he'd yearned for a pair of showy calf-splat boots, he'd never dared buy them.

"How do you do? Everett Potter at your service," the man in the suit said to the two men. "I couldn't help overhear your conversation. If you're looking for land or information about Blood Cut, I'll be in my office in the bank until twelve. I'd be pleased to share my information with you."

"That's very kind of you, Mr. Potter," Julius replied.

"Good day." The banker nodded and followed the other gentlemen out.

After a moment the man dressed in black and the old, red-wigged harridan overdressed in flounces and lace and glass beads passed by without speaking, leaving the restaurant to Julius, Isham, and the cook.

"Mighty good belly-packin' material," Isham said between bites, and Julius nodded agreeably.

"You recognized Rainy Day?"

"Which one was he?" Isham asked deadpan.

Julius rolled his eyes. "It's good that you are not too serious. When we become too serious, we become too nervous, and when the time comes, we miss."

"Can't have that," Isham said, pleased that Rainy Day had not recognized him.

Full and satisfied, they lingered over a cup of coffee. Isham dug in his vest pocket for a gold coin, and his finger touched a piece of folded paper, reminding him of the letter that had been forwarded from place to place until it reached his Texas bank, then was forwarded on to his bank in Monterey, California. It had taken almost a year. Too many months made a cold trail. It was the luck. If he'd stayed in San Antonio, he'd have received the letter from El Paso in a few days, but the writer of that letter hadn't known he'd gone as far west as he could go, hadn't known he'd quit Texas because of the carpetbaggers and the defeated mentality of the people.

After giving the ranch to the carpetbaggers he'd taken his three thousand head of cattle to Abilene, Kansas, sold out, paid off the crew, and ridden west. First to sleepy Santa Fe, then on across the desert to Santa Barbara, where the range was too dry for his custom, on north to foggy Monterey, and one step farther inland to the lovely little valley of San Juan Bautista, where grass grew belly-high on the cattle.

It had been a year's hegira on the lonesome, but he had the money from his herd, and there was enough left to start stocking the ranch on the Pajaro River. With the ranch came a hope for the future, and he'd been growing out of the miasma of the war years, which, despite the valor of the people and the grinding pall of doom wrought by Sherman and Grant, had gradually convinced him that the happy, confident Isham Rye before the war was a figment of a fevered imagination, that the real Isham Rye was maybe one cut above a razorback hog.

That feeling of having mud instead of manhood had gradually fallen away as he grew accustomed to the gentle land and sunny climate of San Juan Bautista. The customs and ambience of the *Californianos* were still there: the barbecue in front of the mission, the rodeos and dances afterward, the girls of various races and nationalities arriving, all vivacious and expanding his vision of life.

He'd almost buried those hard years of the war and the losses in Louisiana and then Texas, almost become an easygoing cattleman with pastures fenced by cheap redwood pickets, was even thinking on a family when the letter came.

He could remember every word of it by now:

Dear Isham,

How are you? I am fine.

No, I'm writing true now, I'm not fine. But I'm not important anymore. Do you remember before the war when we were just kids? How wonderful it was then when we could picnic in the oaks off from your big house and fields, all dressed up and proper until we could get free of them nannys and sneak into the lake. Well, at least I can still relive those memories. And I don't want you to feel you owe me anything for those days, it's the other way, but I just wonder if I might ask you, as a decent man and friend, if you could help me find my little sister, Penelope. She's eighteen now and was working in a clothing store here. Now she's disappeared.

Penny's never been wild like yours truly, but it seems she met a gentleman from New Orleans who thought highly of her and turned her head, as we former southern belles used to say. Penny just left without a word. I have a feeling something's not right about the "southern gentleman" who wears odd-colored boots. Isham, I'm afraid, but I'm going to start turning this town upside down to find her. There's something rotten going on, and I'm not going to lose my only sister to it.

Your friend, affectionately,
Drusilla Waverly

She had thought he was only a couple hundred miles away. She had waited a few days until she decided he wasn't coming and then had gone out on her own looking for Penelope, her sister, or for some relevant information.

After a week or two of making herself a nuisance around the dives of El Paso she was found strangled in an alley. Her purse was gone. It looked like robbery. She was buried in a pauper's field, and the marshal scratched off the murder as just one more incident in the *zona roja.*

The clink of a coin hitting the table brought Isham's mind back to the present. He looked across the table.

"I'm afraid you outfumbled me, Isham," Julius laughed, but there was a serious concern in his eyes.

"Sorry, Julius." Isham felt his face burning. "I was daydreaming."

"It was not a pleasant daydream."

"No. No, it wasn't."

"Would you care to tell me about it?"

"No, I reckon not."

"Oh, you strong, silent Texans," Julius said abjectly, "you carry the whole world's problems on your shoulders as if there was no one to help carry the burden."

"Someday it'll be settled, and then we'll speak of it," Isham said firmly. "I owe you a breakfast."

Isham was tempted to tell the story, but native caution stopped him. It had been drilled into him so strongly that a closed mouth catches no flies, he felt uncomfortable talking about anything, even the weather.

He could see that Julius was a good man. Older, of course, but still vigorous enough and brave enough to jump into a river to save a kid's life.

Maybe he ought to tell Julius about the whoremaster he sought, but he didn't.

5

While Julius and Isham were leaving the restaurant and going next door to the Dew Drop Inn to register, Sam Diggs crouched on his hands and knees studying a film of rock dust that seemed to reveal a hoof track.

Another hour and a vagrant breeze would have obliterated it, but he was in time and could see enough of it to give him a direction to go, and he sighted over the track at a lightning-blasted pine on to the north.

The more he fooled around on his hands and knees, the farther the kid was going. It was that simple. There just wasn't time to track each step; you had to make good guesses and be lucky.

Cutting through the trees, he came to the base of the pine and cursed the bed of resilient pine needles that revealed nothing, but a few feet away he saw where the pinto had picked up his hoof a little slow and dragged the needles in a straight line.

Again he sighted and saw a group of three poplars on a knoll, and he kicked the bay forward. Maybe he wasn't gaining, but he wasn't losing much. He guessed the kid had no more than a ten-minute lead on him, and maybe less. If he pressed hard enough, he'd soon hear the hoofbeats of the running pony, and that would be the end of it because the bay was faster.

As he rode he tried to keep his bearings clear. You didn't want to get turned around in the timber and find yourself going the wrong way.

So far the Blood River was on his left, and that meant he was heading north.

It suddenly occurred to Sam that the kid couldn't go west because of the steep banks of the river. He had to go either north or east. But as the line of timber was so slender, if he went east, he'd be visible in the open prairie, so all Sam needed to do was ride full-tilt ahead and outrun his quarry. He didn't really need to see hoofprints; all he had to do was keep the eastern prairie visible and cover the timber to the river.

The bay was good. Not only strong and with good bottom, he could jump as well, and Sam didn't hesitate to point him directly at a fallen log or small hedge of chokecherries, because the horse responded to the knees and the bridle like a born Irish hunter and seemed to enjoy the setting and the jump, the soaring over and running onward.

The pinto pony couldn't do it, but he was agile enough to dodge obstructions the big bay couldn't. Still, the bay's way was faster, the same as a fast hound following a zigzagging rabbit was faster.

Sam passed the grove of poplars without looking for sign but urged the bay forward, expecting to see or hear the pinto momentarily.

It never happened. He went on another two miles and never heard a whisper or saw a flash of the paint horse. Giving the bay a breather, he realized he'd figured wrong. Logically he should have caught the kid, and he hadn't. So he was wrong. Needed to rethink the whole thing.

He walked the bay back southerly, futilely looking for sign. He crossed from the riverbank a quarter of a mile to the open prairie, and he was sure no running horse had passed by there.

Something wrong with his head, he thought. Getting too old for this game. Time to quit. No, no. You make up for mistakes with experience. Experience counted. A youngster would panic and start running back and forth, or racing out on the prairie, but the veteran would plod along through the trees, crisscrossing until he picked up the trail again.

Yet, at a ledge of sandstone, he almost admitted defeat. There should have been a dust print or scrape on the stone, but it wasn't there. It meant that either the kid had stopped, hidden, then turned back south as Sam rode on by, or he'd turned off into the river.

Sam didn't think the kid could hide that bright pinto.

Therefore, A-B-C, the kid and the pinto somehow went down to the river, and he wouldn't do that unless there was a way out on the other side that no one knew about.

All right. Go slow, Sam. Ride along the river, and you'll sure as hell see the sign if that pony went over the dirt bank fifty feet straight off.

Full of doubt and misgivings, he firmed up his mind and held to the logical path.

Going south at an easy trot, he stayed close to the riverbank.

Nothing. He was almost back to the lightning-blasted pine and full of despair. How could a greenhorn kid elude him so easily? What ever happened to the old-time Sam Diggs, master of all scouting, including tracking Apaches in the Sonoran desert?

He paused to give the bay another breather by a patch of ash and willows. Stepping down, he patted the bay on the neck and looked at the forest. Just a lot of trees. Then he looked at a pine directly in front of him and saw a blaze chopped into it years before. Why? Why here? There was nothing here. No one. Nothing. He moved his vision in an arc, studying each tree and bush as he turned.

There were no more blazes. Perhaps it wasn't a blaze. Suppose a long time ago another tree had fallen against the pine and scabbed the bark. Suppose an Indian had marked the tree as good for pine sap. It could be almost anything. As he finished his 180-degree turn he saw only the brush on the riverbank, and then he saw a silver thread that as he picked it from the brush with two fingers, he found it was not a silver thread. It was a white hair from a paint pony's tail.

The brush seemed too thick to penetrate, but he thought maybe if you led the horse, you could enter the tangle of small trees and get through. To what? To the river, and that was useless. Still, follow the leader. If the kid could do it, ancient, softheaded Sam Diggs could do it, too.

Taking the reins, he led the big horse between two clumps of willows only to face the bole of a mighty chestnut; but turning left, he found a little space to scrape by, and after a while the thick brush opened up into a trail that had been cleared of brush.

How had the kid ever found it?

Savvy kid, but maybe not as savvy as the old silver fox. Sam was smiling, sure that he'd penetrated the last defense of his quarry. Leading the bay along the riverbank, he could hear the water running far below and see how straight off the bank fell.

Where he was going he didn't know, but he was pretty sure the kid would be there.

The trail seemed to edge gradually, dangerously,

over the bank, and Sam wondered if it could be a trap. Lead you down so far and, unable to turn around, you fall the rest of the way and end up with a broken neck.

The sun was hidden behind the tall trees growing on the rich silt where there always was plenty of water. The big horse went down the narrow trail but shied nervously at a big log that had been used to shore up the trail, his head high, moving left and right alertly, as if in the dismal gloom he might catch sight of an ogre or river dragon waiting to drag both horse and rider into its watery den.

The sounds of hooves falling and saddle creaking were swallowed up in the mat of brush and vines and overhanging trees, and the prairie wind was lost in the waterway.

Sam felt as if he ought to be singing or laughing or talking to his horse just to assert his presence in the deep, gloomy quiet, yet it seemed there was some power in the place that would not permit a breaking of the silence. If he'd been a religious man, Sam would have been silently praying.

Still the bay continued down the trail, tossing his head occasionally, but going until they came to the river itself, which Sam had expected to be confined and deep and fast. But the trail came out just above a wide bend of the river where, in times past, floods had carried downed trees and deposited them in the broad bow, then filled in with smaller flotsam followed by the silt dropping from the dammed water, every year higher and higher until there were trees and grass rooted and growing in this delta formed in the crook of the river. The delta had become a small parkland through which the river ran in divided fingers like pretty little brooks, making the crossing easy. A doe and fawn stood tamely to one side munching on willow saplings, and on beyond a crouching bobcat stalked a covey of quail while red squirrels gossiped in the trees overhead.

A little paradise, Sam thought without stopping. Eden.

Coming to the opposite bank, Sam found the fresh prints of the pinto where they angled upward.

The bay buckled down to climbing the trail, and Sam leaned forward over his sweating neck to help him along.

At the top, where the ground became level again, Sam stopped to rest the bay. Here was another tree with an old axe blaze on its side.

Leading the horse, he followed the tracks on foot until he felt certain that the kid was not going to double back or work out a ruse to elude a pursuer. The kid didn't think Sam would find the old trail and crossing. He was thinking he was home free.

Mounting up, Sam followed the clear tracks at a trot. He had the feeling the kid had a particular goal in mind, and that goal wasn't too far away from the way the kid had hurried on without giving the pinto a breather.

The deep riverbank timber was thinning out as he rode west, and he could see through the breaks distant swaths of prairie grass waving in the wind. Slowing the horse to a walk, he considered that he didn't want to just bust into the open without knowing what was out there first.

Halting between two black locust trees at the edge of the timber, he looked out at the gently rolling land covered with deep grass. Here and there were small groups of fat cattle feeding, and they seemed to wear the same brand, indicating their owner lived in the vicinity.

There were a few dips where a house and barn might be located out of sight. Not necessarily hidden, just conforming to the best features of the terrain. If a man could find a hill or swale to break the north wind, he'd best use it.

Avoiding the skyline, Sam stayed on the trail, which turned more north than west until it intersected a worn, rutted wagon road.

Sam knew there were few settlers in the area. Most of the immigrants passed by this area where the winters were killers and the summers close to hell. Just now, in the springtime, it was sweet and growing, and the forage for cattle rich and easy. But it was marginal rangeland, and the few ranches were scattered miles apart.

It came as a surprise then to ride around a knoll and see a log ranch house with a big barn and corrals tucked into a small valley below, divided by a creek.

It must be a fork of the Blood, Sam decided. There was some timber alongside the creek and a hayfield at the lower end.

He thought he could recognize his pinto near the corral, but it was too far away for him to be sure.

Quickly he made a loop that would take him to the lower end of the valley where there was some cover.

Chances were the kid would be docile enough. Sam doubted if there was a mean streak in him, but he was for sure stubborn, and Sam didn't want to lose him again.

Gaining the bottomland, Sam rode directly into the creek and went upstream, concealed by brush and small trees on either side, until he was cut off by a rail fence that crossed the creek. Nothing for it now but to follow along the fence and come in on the ranch house from the back.

It wasn't the regular way a stranger ought to approach a house. Folks didn't go knocking on back doors. You were supposed to come in the front, where everyone could see you first and take a shot at you if they didn't like what they saw.

This way, you were already admitting your guilt before you ever paid the visit. Skulking around like an Injun would get you nothing but a dose of lead poisoning, which, in the light of practical living on the frontier, was exactly what you deserved.

Dismounting by an outbuilding, he left the bay and crept along a picket fence to the corral where half a dozen mustangs snuffled at the dust. His pinto was tied outside. The kid hadn't even taken time to slack the cinches.

Was he in such a hurry to see somebody here, or was he just making sure he could ride out of here fast?

The silence was thick enough to cut with a tomahawk, Sam thought. Quiet as a tree full of owls. How would it be to live out here day after day, year after year, just thinking to yourself?

First thing, you'd be talking to your horse, and next you'd be talking to the fence posts, knowing they wouldn't dispute a word you said.

In his younger days Sam had lived the lonely settler's existence where you lived to work and worked to live, all by your lonesome. He'd done as well as most settlers. At least he hadn't hanged himself from pure lonely misery. He hadn't let the grieving wind sink and blacken his thoughts, but he'd known it wasn't right for a bachelor, and going off to war showed him there was a larger side to life.

So it was that he'd chosen St. Joe as his headquarters. It was a place big enough to be lost in if you chose, or small enough to know everybody in town, and it suited him fine. He kept a dusty office on the second floor of a downtown building that was only a few feet from a redolent, rich saloon where the free lunch was sometimes broiled shrimp, or oysters on the half shell with Creole sauce, or crayfish and pickled eggs.

Passing the corral, Sam reached the barn and worked his way alongside it in the shadows.

He heard voices from the house and held back. He had no plan other than finding Anthony Burlington Barr and hauling him east as fast as possible, but if the kid had friends it wouldn't be so easy. He made sure his .45 was free in its holster and hurried across the open space between the barn and a wash shed directly behind the house.

Pausing for breath, he tried to hear the conversation coming from the front, but it was too far away. He was sure one of the speakers was a woman, a younger woman. Another was a rusty-voiced old man, and yet another was a southern drawl as smooth as peaches and cream.

Staying in the shadows, he gained the back of the main house and again tried to listen to the rising and falling conversation. At least no one was mad about anything; there were no sharp words or sudden exclamations, only the threesome passing the time. Occasionally the young lady's laughter punctuated the dialogue, indicating that everyone was having a good time.

Suddenly he froze as a figure left the concealment of a disused wagon and scurried to the window.

Sam smiled as he recognized none other than harum-scarum Anthony Burlington Barr himself.

He seemed to be singularly distressed as he watched and listened, clenching his fists, swatting at imaginary flies, shaking his head, and at last, giving in to his impulse, Tony hurried around to the front door and knocked loudly.

This gave Sam a perfect cover to sugarfoot over to the same window Tony had just left.

"Why, it's young Mr. Barr," he heard the young lady cry out in surprise. "My goodness, what brings you so far out into the wilderness?"

"Just passing by," Tony said.

Sam could vaguely see the two other men. An old man with a thin, craggy face sat in a chair facing him. The other, facing away, was a man dressed in gray.

"Won't you come in, please?" the young lady said, and she led Tony inside.

She was a yellow-headed and freckled girl, too young and inexperienced to know much of the world, relying instead upon her natural female instincts to cope with this sudden incursion of society.

Neither the old man nor the man in gray rose to shake Tony's hand, and he seemed at loss for what to say.

"I'm sorry to interrupt," Tony stammered.

"Take him into the kitchen and give him a cup of coffee, Nan," the old man said. "I ain't never turned a stranger away yet."

"Mister Packard," Tony burst out, "I didn't come for a cup of coffee. I come to ask your permission to call upon Miss Nan, please."

The old man smiled sourly, turned to the figure in gray, and said, "You'll have to pardon this interruption, Mr. Shado."

"I'm pleased to see your daughter is so popular, which to my eyes is a perfectly natural result of having been born and raised so well."

Nan blushed. "Now, Mr. Shado—"

"As for you, young man," the old man rasped, "I don't reckon you know much about raising cattle, but that's what we do here, and so I reckon you'd just be wasting your valuable time hanging around."

"I can learn, Mr. Packard. All I need is a chance."

"If'n I was to be looking for a son-in-law, which I am not, I'd be looking for somebody a little older and more substantial, if you know what I mean."

"Look, sir," Tony said hotly, "my father—"

He stopped and swallowed. He'd not only been about to reveal his father's financial position, he was about to lean on it. Then he'd realized that he'd broken loose from his father and wanted to be independent and standing on his own two feet.

"Your father?"

"My father . . . doesn't know I'm here."

"Would you mind, Mr. Shado, describing to this young man the nature of your holdings on the west bank of the Blood?"

Old Packard cracked an avaricious smile, as if he not only coveted the property but would like to gather it up in his arms and pet it.

"Well, sir"—Roark Shado shifted his gleaming yellow boots—"I happen to own everything in the bend for several miles except for this parcel on the north end, which is owned by my good neighbor, Mr. Packard."

"And you, boy, what do you own? A horse and saddle? A bedroll?"

"Now, Daddy." Nan smiled. "Don't rub it in."

"Fifty years ago I was the same way," the old man said. "I took my bride from the Tennessee hills on to Texas, and that Texas land wore her down to a nubbin and beat her to flinderjigs, and then it killed her. I swore on her grave Nan would never have to go down that hard road, and that should settle the matter."

"But, wait, sir!" Tony seemed to strangle on his words. "You don't know anything about me, and probably nothing about this man, either."

"Sir?" Roark Shado responded quickly.

"Just a moment, please, Mr. Shado." The old man held up his hand. "Listen to me, young man. Mr. Shado saved my daughter from a danger of the worst kind and has not even asked for one word of thanks, whereas you ride in here like I should kill the fat calf and give you my daughter and my ranch, too. Good-bye."

Sam thought Tony might lose his head and go berserk from sheer frustration. Sam knew the youth's background, where there was money enough to buy everything from here to Blood Cut many times over, but Tony wouldn't come out and say so. He'd be damned if he'd compare his father's fortune with Shado's. The old man and Nan ought to see that he was a good person and take him at face value. It was nobody's damn business whether his family was rich or poor. What was important was how much he loved her.

"Nan," he tried desperately, "Nan, I can take care of you."

"I'm sorry," she said, not revealing any feeling, neither yes nor no, leaving her all the options and him none.

Sam felt a little sick at seeing the innocent youth so madly in love being jockeyed by a girl who already knew the wiles of womanhood, even though she looked like an innocent tomboy totally without guile or deception.

"Get out," the old man growled, starting to rise.

"I can handle it." Roark Shado stood.

"No," the old man said, and he aimed a craggy, twisted finger at Tony. "I said git."

"Yes, sir," Tony said, blushing and shamefaced. Turning quickly to Nan, he asked hurriedly, "Can I see you again?"

"Gosh, Tony, I just don't know what to say," she murmured sadly.

Crouched at the window, Sam felt a wave of sympathy for the misguided youth, and then he heard a boot creak behind him, and then came the solid blow to his head, and he felt nothing at all except a slow black going away.

6

A wizened gnome of a man registered Julius and Isham in the hotel and took their money.

"I'll be wantin' a bath," Isham said, adding another fifty cents.

"I, too," Julius said.

"There's two tubs," the clerk said. "You pour your own hot water from the boiler."

"I'll be in later," Julius said. "First I want to send a telegram."

"Take your time." Isham nodded and went on to the room, where he took clean clothes from his war bag and went on down the hall to the bathroom.

Between two copper bathtubs was a wood stove and a boiler full of steaming water. Isham pumped in a few inches of cold water, then bucketed in enough of the hot to make the temperature a little hotter than tolerable, then undressed and eased his lean, scarred body into the tub. It wasn't an easy fit because the tub was made for average-sized men, but he cherished the warmth and slowly made up some suds from a bar of yellow soap.

He let his head lie back, and the steaming water relaxed his tight, kinked muscles. He seemed to float away on a soap bubble to those halcyon days of his youth in Louisiana, where there were no cares, no thought of trouble or war, only the balmy afternoons spent visiting with friends equally affluent, all pretending to be slightly bored and spoiled, yet all of them wanting to live life to the fullest.

Drusilla Waverly was his age, and her parents' plantation close by. What was more natural than that they should grow up together, learn to ride and dance and accept the courtly manners up to the point where they interfered with the passion of youth? Dru wasn't a girl to hide out in a corner or barricade herself behind the conservative morals of a society that, after all, lived two lives, one to show, one to thrill the blood.

It was all so natural, they felt neither love nor guilt; they felt only the pleasure of being together, joking, teasing, sometimes hopelessly pondering deep philosophical questions.

But Dru was the doer. When she felt the sap rise in her body she couldn't wait, and neither could he refuse.

Was there really true love then, he wondered.

They had certainly thought so at the time, and they repeated that word over and over to each other as they lay under the great sun-dappled oaks by the lake.

Stop it, he told himself, shutting his eyes tightly as if he could blind his mind to those memories.

The war started as if it were a weed sprouted from a stray seed, and it grew rankly on and on until the weed had crowded out the grain and the cotton and the flowers.

He came home with his fresh scars and a devastated spirit to find the whole parish burned, his family and friends dead and gone, and nothing left except the memories. Then, years later, he found the dusty cross leaning over a pauper's grave in El Paso.

She'd wanted to live all of life with joy and passion, and he supposed she'd never backed away from that, but then she was gone, brutally used and strangled. Gone, dust in a dusty field. It wasn't right.

Her sister had to be given a chance. He owed her that.

He'd worked quietly, doled out some money here and there for information, banged the heads of a couple of border-town smart alecks, and found Dru's sister Penny had gone with a fancy-dressed dude to New Orleans. The dude was quite the gentleman, and he seemed to have more money than J. Pierpont Morgan.

He found the stage they'd taken to Brownsville and the coastal steamer they boarded for New Orleans.

At the Hotel La Fitte in the Vieux Carré he saw that they had registered separately and had been given different rooms.

What had this gentleman told Penny to entice her all this way?

Penny had been protected all her life by Dru and had never had the fire and energy of her older sister. She had been a quiet, pretty little girl, just going on with the game, using the rules that had been laid down by people long gone. She would probably put her confidence in almost any southern gentleman if he had a good enough story.

Suppose he'd said that the family plantation was being restored, and he wanted her to see that it was done right. Such a yarn would appeal to her and disarm whatever reservations she might have about traveling with a stranger.

Perhaps the southern gentleman had said it was to be a surprise for Drusilla, and therefore the project must be kept secret. If he was persuasive enough, *southern* enough, she would gladly accept his promise.

The details weren't important—even the scheme itself was unimportant—only that her belief in him was important.

Once he had her in New Orleans, away from all possible help from family or friends, he would close the trap.

In New Orleans Isham had gone to the most exclusive brothels and paid out large sums of money for information until he found the right house. The ladies of the night had been replaced many times since Penelope had been brought there, but the old madam in all her feathered finery remembered her. She'd used another name . . . Blanche . . . that was her. Too bad she had so little talent for conversation with gentlemen and not much sparkle or allure, and so she'd moved on after a few months.

"Where?"

"I have no idea."

"You know. There has to be a route, or several routes. One would be upriver to Baton Rouge, and then on up to the Missouri. Another would go east to the Atlantic and run northward. Another would lead westerly, ending in San Francisco."

"You are a smart one," the old harridan had snorted.

"You know it's true. You know there's an organization of some kind, controlled probably by one person."

"Your guess is as good as mine."

"Just tell me then, your best guess."

"Why don't you try Charleston?"

He studied the old bawd and decided she was lying.

He took the riverboat north to Shreveport, where it was easier to find her trail. She'd stayed in an expensive house for over six months under the name of

Cornelia. The southern gentleman had withdrawn but came to visit occasionally—not only Cornelia; he seemed to have an interest in other demimondaines in the house.

It became a sickening puzzle to Isham, but the pieces slowly came together as he searched for more information.

Often he was deceived: "She died," "She fell down the stairs," "She took the boat to Havana," "She fell in love and went straight."

The women seemed to take pleasure in lying to him, as if they were taking their revenge because he was a man, and therefore responsible for each one's downfall.

The trail led north to St. Louis, where the house was less exclusive and catered to just about anyone who had five dollars in his pocket.

They said she'd turned shabby, had lost heart and hope, become depressed and leaned on a bottle of brandy to see her through the night.

From St. Louis she'd been taken to Wichita, and after a few months they'd shipped her to Abilene.

Following the route, Isham had thought that the organization was treating her and the rest of the sporting girls more like animals than human beings, moving them here and there to make the maximum profit on a critter past its prime in the time left for it to function and have some value as trading goods. It seemed to him that it was more like cannibalism than business, selling the bodies of females, keeping them in line with physical abuse including clubs and whips, and giving nothing back.

The organization seemed to be faceless, almost invisible, but someone kept track of the trade. Someone knew where there was a shortage of females and an abundance of footloose men. Someone knew the big paydays, someone kept the girls moving before they could join their community or find a friend. Someone gathered them as youngsters and broke them to halter.

Some thought it centered in Chicago, others thought it was New Orleans. Most of them didn't care.

Isham had hurried to Abilene, hoping against hope that he wasn't too late.

How long had little simpleminded sister Penelope been sporting? Too long, despite his banging away at the system that was trying to hide her from her past.

Now she traveled under the name of Patricia.

Now she was hustling in the Big Elephant in the railhead town of Abilene, where hundreds of cowboys took their pay and went crazy spending it.

He'd rode down Main, worn down from the dirty trail he'd followed for many months, yet feeling a surge of gladness that he'd end it today, would find her, talk to her, take her as his own little sister to California, where she could start fresh with his support, find a husband, and make a decent life.

He'd avoided the drunken, half-crazed riders who were rebelling against all authority for the few days their wages lasted, wild-haired riders who'd lost their hats, their faces drink-raddled, their eyes insane, their minds transported in a screeching agony by the unfinished and tainted whiskey they imbibed.

There was nothing to do with these men except to wait for them to recover, jail them, knock them unconscious, or kill them.

That they were mild, easygoing, highly skilled stockmen three hundred and sixty days out of the year made no difference in Abilene once they'd been transported into hooraw land by the greasy yellow rotgut.

Isham knew the scene well enough and sympathized with the drunken punchers stampeding up and down the dusty street, howling like wolves in rut, doing saddle tricks, and firing their handguns at most anything that struck their fancy, from the water troughs to the iron weathervanes.

The two-story saloon stood in the middle of the block. Painted on the false front was a western artist's rendition of a blue elephant, trunk raised high, tusks extended.

Inside, Isham had beheld a great noisy barn of a place with a long ell-shaped bar attended by six bartenders dressed in clean starched shirts with fancy armbands holding their cuffs away from their hands. Above the mirror was a life-sized version of Goya's Maja, supine, overweight, and nude except for wisps of voile tastefully covering the most private parts of her anatomy. Isham thought the painter of the elephant and the painter of the Maja were one and the same.

He found elbow room at the bar and ordered a glass of beer.

It was not yet dark, and the overhead lamps had not been lighted. A man on a ladder was replacing one that had been shot out the night before by a cowboy who had mistaken it for the moon.

Off to one side, the poker tables were half empty or half full, depending on how you looked at them, and roughly dressed men wearing big spurs and six-shooters moved about seeking diversion.

Isham had seen a dozen such emporiums, and this one was not much different except it was cleaner and didn't stink so bad, probably because it was new.

Behind him near the door were a few tables where the sporting girls waited for someone to buy a drink and ease their loneliness.

Taking his time, Isham had unobtrusively looked them over. They were already the dregs of the trade. Many months ago he'd started at the top and had searched the houses of lower and lower repute, and here, he realized, was the end of the road for most. When there was nothing else, these would drift away with a snaggletooth buffalo hunter or try to work out something with an Indian down in the Nations. Here were the culls, the cutters and canners.

There were five of them sitting at the tables. Still a little sleepy-eyed, they'd just gotten up, had a cup of coffee or a glass of beer, and gone to work. They didn't expect any business for a couple of hours at least, but the rules were that they had to be ready at five o'clock every day except when the girl was out with the flowers.

Isham had studied them from under the brim of his hat where they couldn't see his eyes.

He was so preoccupied, he didn't notice that a cowboy had staggered up to the bar and bumped him. Without thinking, he'd moved over a few inches, giving the man room.

"What the hell you all doin', knothead—ramming into people?" the cowboy snarled as if he'd been injured.

That tone of voice had penetrated Isham's mind instantly, and he focused on the short trail-fined cowboy whose protruding eyes told him this man was beyond reason.

"Well, by God, ain't you all goin' to say pardon me?" the cowboy had demanded, and men drifted away out of the line of fire.

"Settle down, Tex!" The bartender's yell served only to incite the puncher all the more as Isham remained silent, gauging the resiliency of the other man's hat.

"Ya damn rot ah'm fum Texas, an' meaner'n a tagger en mesquite." The cowboy glared at Isham, his hand hovering over his six-gun.

Isham had decided it was hopeless.

"I tried Texas once." Isham had smiled, pulled his

Colt, swung it down, and laid two and a half pounds of iron on the puncher's head, dropping him like a brain-shot steer.

With the revolver cocked and ready he'd looked around the room for friends of the cowboy, but none were forthcoming as a swamper and deputy marshal dragged the unconscious form outside.

Isham had holstered the Colt, and the room returned to normal. Once again he covertly studied the bar girls at their tables.

From right to left, the first one, short and barrel-shaped, probably claimed she was part Spanish and could be called a señorita, but for sure she was a tough Yaqui Indian. Yet . . . Yet, Isham reproached himself, she, too, had once been a little girl believing that life was all sunrises and rainbows.

Next to her was a tall, heavily built lady with dark features set off by a high mass of yellowish-orange hair. She wasn't a Mexican, maybe, but for sure she wasn't a Swede. She might have been thirty, but she looked sixty despite the paint and powder. At the next table sat two others listening to a man in a well-made gray frock coat whose back was to Isham. The lady on the right was simply gone to fat in volumes, and though her bosom was enormous, it seemed a deck had been constructed under her gaudy dress to support it. Isham thought she'd weigh out at about two-forty. She had a face like a bulldog, with dewlaps under her eyes and a goiter starting to grow on her neck.

The fourth girl vaguely resembled Isham's remembrance of Penny, except her face had broadened and dished so that it seemed almost concave, with her thin, pointed nose hardly breaking the plane. Her cheekbones, mouth, and eyes had sunken, leaving only the little nose to face the world. Her hair was still a mousy brown, but there was no gloss nor shine to it.

Her thin body, which once might have passed as desirably girlish, was now a rack of bones. Isham could not see any expression in her deep-set eyes. He noticed that she filled her glass from a bottle of brandy on the table.

The man in the frock coat was not a customer nor a messenger bringing good news. The four ladies stared at him like oxen watching a campfire die in the night.

In a moment, as the man started to rise, the dish-faced girl's mouth twisted, and she tried to grab his wrist. He was much quicker, and without a farewell or turning to face the bar he straightened his back and walked out the door. Isham had noticed that his boots were calf-splatter yellow.

The dish-faced girl listened as her heavyweight companion muttered an obscene epithet, lifted her glass unsteadily, and drank it down without answering.

She hadn't recognized him as he approached. Why should she? It had been years since he and Dru had tried to elude the pesky little sister, and those years had been savage ones, heavy with death and disaster.

He had taken the chair the frock-coated gentleman had vacated, and he looked into Penny's sunken eyes, which seemed to be as intelligent as slush ice.

"Hi, there, cowboy," she said automatically, "buy me a drink?"

Isham looked at the bulldoggy companion and jerked his head, and she'd said, "Hell, cowboy, don't you know two's better'n one?"

"No," he'd replied flatly, and she moved over to the other table without protest.

He'd signaled a waiter and said, "What do they call you?"

"Patricia."

"I knew a Patricia over in Tennessee once."

"I'm from Louisiana. Where you from?"

"Happens I'm from Louisiana, too."

The waiter brought her a glass of real brandy, not tea, and a glass of beer for Isham.

"What part?" she asked by rote and without interest.

"My folks had a plantation called La Belle near St. Croix."

It had seemed to go right by her as if she were deaf or her mind was completely burned out.

"Sounds right pretty."

"Our neighbors had a plantation called The Cedars."

"I been to New Orleans," she said, unblinking. "Thanks for the drink."

"My pleasure. Over at The Cedars was two brothers that went and died at Gettysburg, and two sisters."

"Where you from, big fella?" she'd asked again, as if she hadn't heard a word he'd said.

"One was Drusilla, and the kid sister was named Penelope."

"That's nice. You want to go upstairs?"

"Maybe that'd be better, Penny," he'd said, feeling a terrible fear in his mind. Maybe he was too late. Maybe she'd made the big jump and couldn't turn around anymore.

He'd followed her slender form out a side door to a stairway that creaked as they went up.

The stairway opened onto a hall with unpainted wooden doors every few feet. She'd opened the second door on the left, and he'd followed her inside a small cubicle that held a commode and a bed and little else.

Hardly pausing, she'd tugged at her bodice and at the same time said dully, "That'll be five dollars, cowboy."

"Listen to me, Penny. I'm Isham Rye"—he put the

money on the dresser—"Isham Rye. I used to court your sister, Dru. Remember me?"

She wasn't paying attention as she struggled with the buttons on her blouse.

He'd come close to her and taken her trembling hands.

"Penny, we're leaving here. I want to take you to California."

"California? They say that's a far piece. Clear over the shinin' mountains. I just don't think I'd like to travel that far."

"Penny," he said softly.

"Mister, I reckon you got the wrong girl. My name is Patricia. I come from New Orleans. And I just don't have all night to talk."

"Penny, it's Isham. Try to remember, back before the war."

"Mister, are you payin' just to talk? Some do, you know. Some just like to watch a girl undress. Some want extras. It's all right with me, just tell me what's your pleasure."

"I'll take my time talkin', Penny." Isham had had to grip his big hands together to keep from yelling while at the same time he felt he was suffocating with a nameless terror, and even then a slow sorrow was building in his chest as he tried to reach into Penny's mind.

"Remember how we used to sail little boats and skinny dip in the lake? You and me and Dru? I got a letter from Dru. 'Course, it took more'n a year before it found me, but I came to El Paso looking for you."

"Mister," she'd murmured vacantly, "I meet a lot of strange fellows in this line of work, but I reckon you must take the prize."

Suddenly someone rapped hard on the door, and a coarse woman's voice yelled, "Time's up. Get on your pants and don't be sneakin' extras."

Penny shuddered at the sound of the voice and fumbled with her blouse again.

"Penny, can I take you out of here right now, or do I have to buy you out? It's no difference to me, just so we get started."

"Mister, I can't leave. I tried depending on men a few times, and all I got for it was a lot of bruises and a broke nose."

"Penny, listen, please. Trust me. Soon as you can quit the brandy and the laudanum, your memory'll come back."

"That's one thing you can bank on, mister. I ain't quittin' nothin'."

She'd giggled vacantly like a dazed girl. "Men are always such do-gooders . . . up to a point."

"It's me. Isham. Isham Rye. Remember?"

"Isham Rye. Funny name." Her voice had changed as if the name had finally broken through a wall. "I remember you and Dru hidin' from me out at the lake, leaving me to sail the boats alone, and I could guess what you was doin'. Isham Rye. Yes, I recall a boy with that name."

"Let's get out of here, Penny, right now."

"Now, Isham, I never was known for bein' smart, but even I can figure that I have done hit bottom." She'd giggled again. "There ain't no way left but up."

She rose from the bed, opened a drawer, removed a worn fur muff, and incongruously put her hands inside.

"What was the name of the man who took you to New Orleans?" Isham had asked, cold sweat running down his spine.

"Isham, I'd like you to go downstairs and wait for me. I need to fix myself up some."

"You won't need the muff in California," he'd said with relief, going to the door.

There were tears in her eyes, and she'd said softly,

"Bein' a kid sister's never any fun, then the war, then the poverty . . . I thought somehow when Rory came my time for happiness had finally arrived."

"Rory?"

"But there never was a day I'd call happy. Even the brandy and the laudanum can't change it."

She wasn't sobbing or whispering, only silently weeping beads of tears that coursed her empty face and fell to the floor.

She'd squeezed her hands in the fur muff and hunched her shoulders as if she were cold. "Please, Isham—give me a minute to make myself right."

"I'll be waitin'," he'd said, and he stepped out into the hall. Hardly had he closed the door when a shot had come loudly through it.

Quickly he'd turned, charged back inside, and seen her crumpled on the pine floor, a heavy-caliber one-shot muff gun in her hand, a black powder-crusted wound in her right temple. No question but that she had died instantly.

Kneeling beside her, he touched her face and murmured, "Sail away . . . sail away, little girl." Then, as he heard boots climbing the stairs, he'd gone out in the hall to explain, but no one paid him any attention.

The room was cleared, cleaned, and in use by the time he'd ridden to the edge of town and headed north.

7

Rory," he said aloud as the door banged closed.

"How is the bath?"

Julius's voice broke the spell, and his mind returned to the living present.

"I'm feelin' cleaner," Isham responded, feeling that he had passed a point and put the grimness of Dru's and Penny's deaths behind him.

Rory was the future.

Kill Rory.

As Julius poured his own bath and undressed, Isham noticed that he wasn't nearly as fat and paunchy as his rumpled clothes made him appear. No question but that he had muscle enough to wrestle a bull or hold his own with younger men. A round, puckered scar in his upper right chest and another on the thigh attested to his frontier experience.

"Bullets or arrows?" Isham asked out of curiosity.

"Both of them come from bullets." Julius eased into the steaming tub. "The one in the shoulder was from a bushwhacker with a rifle. Knocked me clear out of my stirrups."

"Catch him?"

"Oh, yes," Julius replied happily. "He made the mistake of coming to admire his marksmanship."

"And the other?"

"Ah, a man tried a fast draw on me. Even after he was dead he pulled the trigger. He would have been proud of himself."

"Why?"

"Why? Because he was the only man ever shot me face to face." Julius laughed.

"Send your telegram?"

"Yes, now my patient wife knows I have arrived safely and won't worry no more."

"Reckon I'll have a look at the town." Isham climbed out of the tub and dried himself off with a rough towel.

"I see you have your own scars," Julius said.

"Mine are from the war. You can get two or three in one day that way." Isham smiled.

"Yes, and worse, you don't even know who has hurt you."

"Or the other way either." Isham nodded. "It's not a manly way to fight if you don't have any idea of who you're killin'."

"That's so." Julius shrugged and slumped in the suds.

"If it ain't man to man, I ain't ever goin' again," Isham concluded as he stepped out into the hall, leaving Julius to his own thoughts.

Julius lay comfortably in the hot, soapy water, wondering if his plan would work. Definitely the telegram would go to his wife, and if nothing happened, she would immediately run over to the U.S. marshal's headquarters and give it to the captain. There the captain would read: "Arrived safely, looking for ranch near here." He would understand the simple code to mean that Julius was close to finding and arresting his man.

If he had needed help, he would have added, "Need your approval."

The routine was fairly simple so long as no one discovered he was a U.S. marshal. He needed only to pretend he was a rancher ready for the picking, and they would do the rest.

They should have read his telegram by now, which would lend veracity to his story.

How much could he count on big Isham Rye? There was much going on behind his placid appearance. The scars, the sure hands, the heavy shoulders all added up to a man of powerful strength and courage, yet there was another factor that disturbed him.

Julius couldn't put his finger on it exactly, but it was in Isham's eyes and the set of his jaw, as if his spirit were in turmoil, his convictions confused, his idealism shaken. This man was close to putting himself outside of human society. This man was close to turning his back on the world and making his own laws and going on his own way without caring about his fellow men. Some deep tragedy was eating him inside out.

He needed to know more about Isham Rye, because if Isham Rye twisted and went off the deep end, he must be prepared to kill him.

Julius's way of working was not by beating men until they revealed the secret, but rather to put himself in the other's place and imagine how he'd feel in the set of circumstances. In that way he could work back in time and intuit how the man had felt at the time of the crime and how he had reacted, and how he would behave under stress in the future.

It was entirely possible that Isham Rye, if given a chance, would murder his quarry in cold blood.

There was an awesome hatred in that man's soul. A hatred that could turn into barbaric revenge with one wrong word.

What had he said? "I mean to skin him first, then whittle off a few choice parts before I salt him down and put him on the fire."

There had been nothing humorous in his tone of voice.

Julius shivered in spite of the warm water and the sweat on his forehead. Heaven help him if they were both after the same man.

Julius thought of his wife and wished she were with him. Although she was not the slim-waisted beauty he had married years before, she had developed such a sense of fun even in the chaos of seven children running about, each one wanting attention, that they all had been infected by her jolly way of going on day by day so that he loved and respected her all the more.

He missed the kids, too, missed their climbing over him when he sat down to relax with a cold glass of beer, missed them bringing him their projects for his approval, missed their kisses and their individual and collective beauty. What a happy, harmonious family his dear wife Susanna had given him. He must remember to find some gold earrings for her.

The only fly in the soup was his job.

El Paso was not in his district, but if there was a serious crime, it was his job to help bring the guilty party to justice. There was also a hundred square miles around Fort Worth that he had to patrol and keep the peace in, and always he tried to keep himself out of the public eye.

This case had built slowly from a woman's unsolved murder in an alley in El Paso to the disappearance of other women, into a case of land fraud, and perhaps more, such as blocking public roads, extortion, and murder.

There was little hard evidence, except that a certain man had been seen in the area in most cases, a southern gentleman whose style of life seemed above suspicion.

The attorney general was concerned that this man and his cohorts might try to establish a power base in the middle of the public lands, a circumstance that would be politically embarrassing and no doubt reopen the wounds between the north and south. This was something that the new administration was very anxious to heal and put behind it.

Julius McCrea was the natural agent to assign to the case because he was from outside El Paso, and few people knew him to be a U.S. marshal.

"Julius, we want to put this fire out before it gets any bigger," the captain had said.

"I don't understand what connects Blood Cut to El Paso. It's too far away and too small."

"It's small now, but these men are ambitious, with big ideas. I wouldn't be surprised if they tried to raise a militia of southerners, make an alliance with the Sioux and Cheyenne, and hold back western expansion for another ten years."

"You're speaking of the same people who traffic in women along the border?"

"We're not sure. Only that there are ties between the two. They are clever as hell about not leaving any witnesses behind."

"I'll be ready in an hour, Captain."

"Listen, Julius, your job is only to penetrate the group, not to arrest them. Telegraph me when you're ready to round them up, and I'll get help to you from the nearest federal agencies, including the army, if necessary."

"Yes, sir."

Julius had saluted and ridden home to gather his

traveling gear and explain the telegram relay system to Susanna. From there he'd taken the long trail north.

Now here he was, lazily lying in a hot bath while the criminals walked about the land unmolested.

Yet this bath was part of the deception to throw them off his path and hide his identity. They would be watching the moves of every stranger in town. They had not gotten this far without being careful. If he was not even more careful and clever, a telegram would come to his wife saying, "We deeply regret to inform you . . ."

Half asleep, Julius didn't hear the door open, but he looked up when he heard it close.

Big powder-burned Patch, not drunk, but mean in liquor, came close, glanced at Julius in the tub, then picked up his pants from the bench and went through the pockets.

"Hey, there, mister, those are my pants," Julius protested.

Patch glared at him and, finding Julius's wallet, opened it and counted the money. Then he studied the card that identified him as a voting citizen of Texas, and a card from the Stockman's Association stating he was a member in good standing, and another from the Cattle Breeders' Federation, also attesting to his profession.

Patch went through the rest of the clothing and found nothing of interest.

"Leave my stuff alone and get out of here!" Julius yelled angrily.

"Who are you, mister? It don't make sense an old granger like you would come up here to settle down."

"Listen to me, you hog," Julius replied, "I personally wouldn't live within a hundred miles of you, but if I can find the right property at the right price, I'll send up my cowboys with a herd of cattle."

"Who the hell you think you are callin' me a hog?"

"Who are you working for?"

"I don't work for anybody," Patch growled.

"My guess is you don't work and never have," Julius retorted.

Julius was torn between emerging naked from the tub to defend his pants or simply sinking under the water in mortification at being caught in such a predicament.

Of the two, he chose to stand up and fight, but it wasn't that simple. The suds were slippery, and he had to steady himself with both hands to climb out of the tub, giving Patch an opportunity to shove him back down into the water again.

Patch liked the odds.

"I never beat up a buck-naked man before." He grinned, leaning over the tub. "Trouble is, you ain't washed your fat face yet."

Seizing Julius by the hair, he plunged his head under water until Julius, by sheer muscle, scrabbled loose and managed to get a breath of air.

"You ain't clean yet, fat man." Patch laughed and shoved Julius's head under again.

Julius tried to pry Patch's big hands loose, but he could get no purchase in the bathwater, and he wondered if all this was happening because of the gray hair he'd noticed in the mirror the day he'd left home.

In sudden rage he broke Patch's hold, swung a leg over the rolled edge of the tub, and threw himself onto the floor, where, if he could get to his feet soon enough and get his eyes open, he could fight.

He pawed at his eyes, trying to get rid of the fiery soap inflaming them, and he didn't hear the door open, nor Isham come in.

Isham almost smiled as he sized up the situation. Poor Julius on his knees, scrubbing at his eyes. Patch standing close by, ready to clout him if he got to his feet. The disturbed clothing on the bench. Clearly

Patch was enjoying his rare good luck at catching his opponent at a complete disadvantage.

"Can anybody play?" Isham asked mildly, and Patch, hearing his voice, whirled and went for his gun.

But Isham had already sprung forward, uncorking a mighty right hand as he came, a right hand that skewed Patch's keglike head around, followed by a sharp left hook that caught Patch on the right side of his bull neck with such velocity that the nerves in Patch's right arm were momentarily paralyzed, and the gun fell to the floor.

Patch covered up and retreated, trying to regain his bearings, at the same time hoping Isham would make a wrong move. He wanted Isham to throw another right he could parry and then grab the wrist, twist, and either break the arm or dislocate the shoulder—it didn't make much difference. Once he had his opponent crippled he could take his own good time in stomping his guts out.

Isham, though thirty pounds lighter than Patch, knew better than to close with the bigger man.

"Hit him, Isham!" Julius yelled, wrapping a towel around his midsection.

Patch let his right arm droop as if it were still numb and hid his jaw behind his left arm.

Instead of coming back with another right cross, Isham stepped forward and double-hooked him in the belly with his left, driving the wind out of him.

Patch bounced off the wall and dropped his guard.

Isham threw the right then, and Patch saw his chance. Whirling to the right, he avoided the blow, grabbed Isham's wrist, and twisted.

Isham went to his knee to save the arm and rolled on ahead of Patch's intended rotation. He came to his feet and jammed the first two fingers of his left hand in Patch's eyes.

Patch yelled and relaxed his hold, which would have

ended in a hammerlock, and in rage he swung a sudden right hand that clipped Isham's jaw, sending him reeling back across the slippery floor.

Julius had wisely retrieved Patch's gun from the floor and backed clear.

Patch rushed like a maddened bull after Isham and clobbered him again with a roundhouse left that nearly lifted him out of his boots.

Isham managed to duck the next one and parry the one after, giving his head time to clear. As Patch bulled forward again Isham slid aside and brought an overhand right down on Patch's cheekbone. Patch turned and dived at Isham, trying to tackle him and grip him in his apelike arms.

Isham moved aside and kicked Patch in the kidney as he went by.

Patch forgot all skill and strategy, and in a grunting rage he came to his feet and rushed again, his arms spread wide as if he could gather Isham into them and then crush him to death.

Desperately Isham stepped forward on his left foot, pivoted, and—using all the force of his wheeling shoulder—sent his right fist to Patch's exposed jaw. Fist and jaw collided with a sharp crack that sounded like a maul smacking a wedge.

Isham's right arm went numb to the elbow, but his left hook came across instinctively, turning Patch's iron skull back the other way.

As the big man with glazed eyes and open mouth flopped like an undercut pine tree, Isham stepped back and breathed deeply. He looked at his right fist and flexed his fingers. A man with a broken hand in this country was close to being dead.

If that hand didn't function perfectly, didn't seize the grips of his .44 exactly in balance, and the thumb didn't bring back the hammer to full cock as the hand lifted, so that when the sights coincided on the target, the first finger could squeeze the trigger without disturbing the aim of the long gun barrel—if all those pieces didn't function as smoothly as a greased eel, then you'd lose your life.

For sure, that hand was as precious as both eyes in this violent land.

The knuckles were puffing up and seemed to operate a tad stiffly, but they'd have to make do.

Patch was out cold.

Julius dressed quickly.

"What should we do with him?"

"A hog like that oughta have one bath in his life." Isham smiled. "You take his feet."

The two of them hoisted the big man and swung him back and forth as Isham counted, "One, two . . . three!" and they tossed him into the tub.

Patch's eyes opened and rolled down as his mind struggled through the fog.

By the time he regained full consciousness Isham and Julius were walking into the livery stable. Julius found his Spanish mules in one large stall and saw that they had hay and water, while Isham checked on his own claybank, making sure he had been grained.

The stableman, an old cowpuncher who gimped along on a crooked leg that had been broken in a stampede and badly set, had been forced to take whatever work he could get.

"Much horse," he said as Isham ran his hand down the horse's foreleg and lifted his hoof to check the shoe and frog. "I gave him an extra dollop of corn for breakfast."

"I noticed you rubbed him down, too. I appreciate that," Isham said, and he put a silver dollar in the man's hand.

"Wasn't nothin'." The old puncher smiled. "I like to dress up a good horse when I see one, and that ain't so often."

"You see about everybody that crosses the river, don't you?" Julius asked.

"I'm the first on this side."

"I'm curious if you could possibly not see six hundred beeves pass by." Julius smiled and winked at the old puncher.

"Mister, they don't call me Gimpy for nothing. I'm on the straight, but I got to live. When I get a notion there's something going by that ain't any of my business, I go back into my room and think about my future."

"So you couldn't see a herd of cattle go by?"

"No, sir, I wouldn't. If you was old and crippled up, you'd figure that out mighty fast," Gimpy said defensively.

"I'm not traveling like a colt anymore myself," Julius said bleakly, "and when a man gets gray he's just as crippled as you."

"Depends on his trade," Gimpy answered, his keen eyes on Julius's face. "A lawyer or a merchant, he can go soft and it won't bother him much, but when a horse thief grows soft he's set for hangin'."

"And a fightin' man"—Isham smiled—"when his cinch starts gettin' frayed he better learn to run."

8

Sam Diggs groaned and retched before he tried opening his eyes. His head felt like the inside of a bass drum in a Fourth of July parade.

He felt the thundering in his head, and he was afraid if he opened his eyes the trombones would start blasting away.

Where was he?

Who brought me?

"Whyn't we jes throw him in the hog pen?"

"Maybe later."

The voices came raggedly into his consciousness. One of them sounded like old man Packard. The other must be the sneaky jasper that had coldcocked him.

"Reckon he's dead?"

"No, but you crowned him over hard."

"If I don't get 'em the first whack, I'm a goner."

They both chuckled at that joke, the humor of which escaped Sam Diggs, who was trying to decide whether he could open his eyes or was permanently blind.

On the second try they opened, and he saw the two

old men floating around above him as he tried to focus his eyes.

"Comin' to."

"'Bout time."

"What you doin' here, mister?"

"Good question," Sam replied slowly. "What are you doing here?"

"We live here. You don't."

"You always hit strangers over the head?" Sam played for time, trying to get his body connected to his brain, something that seemed impossible just then.

"Sneaks and spies we do," old man Packard said. "What're you lookin' for?"

"I'm tryin' to take that young swain off your hands."

"He's gone. Promised to come back, though." The other man chuckled, fondling a length of lead pipe.

Sam decided they were brothers who between them and occasional outside help could run the ranch.

No wonder the girl wanted out.

No wonder she didn't know anything.

Sam sat up very slowly, holding his head in his hands, and the two old men stepped back.

"What's the matter with that kid?" Nan's father asked.

"Nothin' that a little lovin' care wouldn't cure."

"Who is he?"

"Just a brush popper, a no-good kid tryin' to get your ranch for nothin'." Sam smiled. "Born a orphan bastard, he has a congenital condition."

"You don't say!" the old brother exclaimed. "We best boil everythin' he touched."

"Yeah, boil your daughter first," Sam muttered, getting to his feet. "Now I'm goin' back and find my horse, and I hope I never see either one of you again anywhere, any time."

"How come you put your horse out back?" old man Packard asked sharply.

Sam saw the trap in time. The old man was worried about someone discovering his river crossing.

"I circled around," Sam lied. "Figured to come in on the blind side."

"Mister, you git. If you or that lunatic ever come back here, you're goin' to end up in the hog pen."

Nan came out on the porch and, with her hands on her hips, watched him ride by. Sam wondered what had happened to the southern gentleman she fancied so much. His first thought was that she deserved him, but his second thought was more sympathetic. The girl, raised out here in the middle of nowhere by a couple squirrely old men, had no idea of what was real in the outside world and what was false.

Sam found the main trail that paralleled the river and let the bay go smoothly in an easy canter.

The kid would be in town. He couldn't go anywhere else, being tied as he was to Nan Packard. He'd hang around day after day with his tongue hanging out, waiting to get a glimpse of her, hoping that she might relent and give him the royal nod of approval. So went the world of the young, he thought, and he considered himself lucky to have lived through that period of his life with minimal damage to his spirit.

Yet when the time is gone, it's gone. There was a time in there, about between the time he was twenty and thirty, when he felt he was the master of his world, except most of it was wasted slogging through the war. He'd been really strong then, and maybe it was that strength that had brought him through the war—but hell, a man wanted to do more with his energy than just survive. He'd accomplished nothing in the war. No one had, except the profiteers. Of course, the blacks were freed, but the government centralized, and the profiteers had stolen all the money so's they could enslave the whites, even the children, in their mines and factories.

Four years he'd marched and fought until there was neither rations nor hope, and when he'd come home he was too restless to go back to studying law.

What would become of him? If he let an old man sneak up on him, it was about time he settled down behind a desk and hired some young hotshots to do the leg work and take the head knocks.

He had no family left and few real friends. Why not get on a ship and set off for that Typee Island that Melville wrote about? You didn't need any money there, not even clothes, because it was always warm, and you just picked your dinner off a tree.

What's going to happen to you, Sam, he thought, if you don't find out what you want? You just goin' to drift along until some old man hits you with a lead pipe a little too hard?

No. Find the kid and take him back to his daddy; take that money to San Francisco, still a young city, and ride it out to the end.

Out there everybody lived to be sixty, seventy years old.

He smiled at his thoughts and himself and wondered if this kind of worrying happened to everybody approaching forty. Surely he wasn't that unique or different from anyone else. He'd just had his head banged a few extra times.

Coming into town, he let the bay walk down the main street, looking for his pinto. Coming to the livery table at the crossing, he saw Julius and Isham Rye talking to the crippled liveryman.

Dismounting, he gave the reins to Gimpy and said, "Take good care of him, please."

"Corn?"

"I'd rather oats, if you have any."

"Costs extra."

"He's worth it."

"Find your boy?" Julius asked.

"Found him and lost him," Sam replied.

"He came through town goin' west a few minutes ago," Isham said. "Wasn't hurryin'."

"He'll be back. There's nothin' out there on the prairie that will doctor his particular ailment," Sam said. "I'll wait for him."

"She take to him?" Isham asked.

"Yes and no." Sam smiled.

"Like a female."

"Exactly right. You know anything about a southern gentleman who's strayed north?"

"Seen him, that's all," Julius said carefully.

"Why?" Isham asked.

"Somethin' coyote about him. He's about got that girl corraled and takin' sugar from his hand."

"Wears calf-splat boots?"

"That's him." Sam nodded.

"He drove his buggy in a little after the kid came through."

"He have a business in town?"

"That's a pack of questions, Sam," Isham said. "What's important about him?"

"I think he's weasel smart," Sam said. "I have a hunch he's the he-boar in this cabbage patch."

"Possible. We're fixin' to call on the local banker. Want to come along?"

"What's the occasion?" Sam asked dubiously.

"He's goin' to talk about property, and we figure to find out what his plans are for us." Julius chuckled.

The bank was small enough that Everett Potter could sit at his desk near the back wall and keep bis eye on the teller and anyone coming in to do business.

He stood and stepped around his desk to greet the threesome.

Word had already gotten around town how the cowboy had knocked out big Patch, and that made him interesting. From the telegram he'd sent, the fat man seemed to have money of his own or backers, and the citified hound dog had killed Virgil the other night, proving he was a lot faster than he looked.

The paunchy, short banker in his worsted business suit considered how he could use them to his profit as he made a flinty smile of welcome.

"Come, set down here. I don't have no secrets, so I don't need no fancy office," he said, laying on the corn-pone dialect.

"Mighty kind of you, sir," Julius said, settling into a chair in front of the banker's desk.

"Just call me Everett. I don't stand on ceremony, I just like to get to the bottom of things right off and help out all I can."

"We aren't exactly lookin' for a loan," Isham said, "just a little information about the country around here."

"And you, Sam?"

"I'm at loose ends," Sam said, "and tired of ramblin'."

"You've come to the right place. We're smack in the way of the immigration trains. They all have to cross the river here, refit, buy supplies, find services. Why, Blood Cut is a wide-open opportunity for anybody from a preacher to an embalmer."

"Well, I ought to fit in there somewhere," Sam sighed.

"Now, there's no land left on the river, of course,

but just west of town, less'n two miles, it's open range."

"Water?"

"There's a few springs and a creek or two," the banker said, not batting an eye as he stretched the truth. "I can handle all the paperwork if you find something you like."

"What I'd like"—Sam chuckled like he was making fun of himself—"what I'd like is to find another crossing of the river."

"Well, that's a fine, get-rich-quick idea, but impossible. The river's narrow and deep and runs fast everywhere but right here."

"That's my luck," Sam muttered lugubriously. "Always a dollar short and a day late."

"Any of you men have a special trade or skill?" the banker asked carefully.

"I can shoe my own horse," Isham said, "but I wouldn't call myself a blacksmith."

"I might be interested in a large piece of grazing land. My backers don't want anything small," Julius said.

"What would you call small?"

"Down in Texas, a small ranch is about ten square miles."

The banker sputtered and choked.

"We'd want about forty square miles of good grass and water and a place to put a meat-packin' shed and a railroad. Of course, we'd bring up some Mexicans to process our beef."

"Of course." The banker forced a smile as he tried to absorb the grandiose idea. "I'm sure we can work somethin' out. What about you, Isham?"

"Me, I'm just a rannie tired of lookin' at the hind end of a steer all day."

"I seem to detect southern accents in your speech," Potter said slowly, looking from one to another.

"I'm from Louisiana," Isham said.

"Texas," Julius nodded.

"Missouri," Sam said.

"I'm from South Carolina myself, the heart of the Confederacy. The reason I asked is that we go out of our way to bring compatriots to Blood Cut."

"We?" Sam asked.

"The other southern gentlemen here in town. May I inquire as to your military service?"

"I rode with Jeb Stuart all the way to Gettysburg and back," Isham said softly.

"I served with Hood's Texans," Julius said.

"I went over and joined up with Longstreet's artillery," Sam said. "We were there."

"Fine, fine," the banker said effusively. "For veterans of the Grand Army we offer special inducements, cash or land, whatever is needed to build up a citizenry capable of defending our borders."

"Mighty interestin'," Sam said, his hound-dog eyes glinting.

"The Yankees think they can control the whole country from Washington, D.C. We aim to show 'em they're wrong."

"You're figurin' on some sort of militia?" Julius asked.

"Why not? The Mormons have taken a huge territory and raised an army to protect themselves against the corruption of Washington, D.C., so why can't we southerners do the same thing?"

"This here financial inducement—is that like so much per month?"

"Depends," the banker replied, looking at his pink fingernails. "We are paying the central core of the new militia. I'm afraid you've encountered a few of them already."

"Patch, and that gunsel Virgil." Sam nodded. "Figures."

"They earn their way doing what they do best." The banker smiled like a bird of prey.

"You mean like rustling Yankee cattle and such." Julius returned the smile.

"They're a rather good investment." The banker nodded. "I'm sure we could put you in close to the top, with your experience."

"We're just feeling our way, speaking only for myself," Julius replied. "What other inducements are there?"

"Well, say you need cattle to stock your ranch. We can sell cattle for practically nothing to our friends."

"Say, now, you boys sure have covered every rat-hole in the barn!" Isham grinned. "What about the simple pleasures of life?"

"The town is ours, don't you see?" The banker smiled. "Everything in the Bucket, including the female companionship, is discounted to our people."

"I'd think you'd already be overrun by southerners stampedin' up here," Sam said.

"We're not after a mob. We're trying to select the best of the best. We want men with pride in their heritage."

"I can qualify." Isham grinned. "Let's get right over to the Bucket and have a hoo-raw!"

"Not so fast, son." Potter held up his hands. "We like to have our people prove themselves first."

"Well, that's the normal story of my life," Sam said sadly.

"Just tell us what the initiation rules are, and we'll see what we can do," Julius said.

"Ah, yes." Potter clasped his hands together, making a bridge for his chin to rest upon. "There's no hurry. Let me speak to those in charge and see if there is some action forthcoming that would serve to bring you aboard."

"I take it no one would mind if I rode on west and looked over the range land?" Julius rose to his feet.

"Not at all. Welcome to the New South."

"I had a little altercation with a couple old mavericks north of town. Are they in on this, too?" Sam asked, getting to his feet.

"Um"—the banker hesitated—"let me just say they come from the state of Maine, where they grew potatoes."

"It figures." Sam nodded and touched the lump on his head. "Hopeless cases."

"I will be in touch with you," the banker said as they went out the door.

"I could use a drink even if I have to pay Yankee money for it," Sam said.

"Let me buy," Julius said.

"My idea is to have three drinks. That way we don't have to fight over the bill." Isham chuckled, and, three abreast, the big men strolled across the street to the entrance of the Bucket Saloon.

Although not so crowded as it would be later on in the evening, there were still plenty of customers bellied up to the bar. Sam noticed toothy Mason was at the end, drinking by himself.

"I see the southern infantry private at the end of the bar," Sam murmured. "I wonder where the sergeant is."

"I'd say Sergeant Patch is looking for a dentist." Julius smiled and ran his finger over Isham's barked knuckles.

"That's the best news I've had so far today. Don't tell me any more, or I'll get so puffed up I might forget where I am," Sam said.

"Yes, that'd be dangerous," Isham agreed. "But I've got another idea that some of the army is out west wet-brandin' cattle, while the rest is on south, bringin' in more."

"You don't think Patch and Mason make up a army?" Julius asked.

"No, not even including Colonel Rainy Day. There's got to be some owlhooters hid out somewhere this side of the river that can handle a herd."

"How many you suppose?" Sam asked.

"Well, Quantrel only needed about forty to make his brigade," Isham said. "I saw them one time up by Sedalia. Foulest dregs of the Confederacy to ever carry the Stars and Bars."

"This bunch will be no better." Sam tasted his beer and looked about the room, hoping to see the kid. He saw no one he knew except Rainy Day at the far corner table, his back to the wall, laying out a game of solitaire.

Even as he watched, the southern gentleman in the calf-splat boots arrived with an elegantly dressed lady at his side.

"There's the top brass," Sam murmured.

"New sporting girl," Julius noticed.

"Maybe he has a glandular problem," Sam said.

"He's goin' to have a heart problem right soon." Isham's eyes were suddenly blazing.

"Steady on, lad," Julius murmured under his breath. "There's more than him in this."

"Who's boss?" Sam asked in a whisper.

"Not Day. He's boss when it comes to killin', but he never plans more'n a day at a time."

"Potter or that Roark Shado, then?" Sam asked.

"Roark?" Isham repeated. "Rory? Yes, that's the scut for sure." Again his face set in cold hatred, his fist balled up into a rock.

"He's not going anywhere, lad," Julius murmured softly. "Patience."

"What's got you so roddy, Isham?" Sam stared at him.

"I've taken a dislike to that Roark feller. Now that I know it's him," Isham growled, "I'd as liefer kill him like a yeller dog right now."

"Julius's right. Best get an idea how big this yellow-jackets' nest is before tearin' into it."

"I'm holdin' it down, friends," Isham gritted, "but that's the bird I been lookin' for, and I mean to have him."

Julius understood it then. This was the man Isham wanted to skin, carve, salt, and roast.

How much evil could a man do to deserve such a punishment?

"Isham, Sam, I want you to know something before we get too far off the reservation."

"Shoot."

"I'm a U.S. marshal, and I can't condone murder no matter what you call it."

"I'm not goin' to murder him," Isham said. "I'm goin' to make coyote bait out of him, fair and square."

"If you have any evidence, I can arrest him."

"And then take on the army of the New South?" Isham retorted. "Listen to me, Julius, when I see a rattlesnake, I shoot it. I don't go ask permission first."

"Have you any evidence? Witnesses? Anything?"

"My witnesses are dead."

"Let it lie," Sam said, trying for calm. "We're talkin' more than we're listenin'."

"Sam's right." Isham nodded. "I'm sorry I got so edgy."

"No doubt you have reason," Julius said.

"I sure don't feel comfortable discussin' coyotes right here in the middle of their den," Sam said.

"Agreed." Julius laid out the money and led the way to the door.

Outside he wiped the sweat off his round face with a bandanna.

"You boys trying to make an old man out of me?" Julius sighed.

"You forty yet?" Sam asked.

"Forty-two."

"I hope you make forty-three."

9

As the trio made their way out of the saloon Roark Shado turned slightly in order to watch them from the corners of his eyes. It was a lesson he'd learned long ago, and it had become such a strong habit that he couldn't look a man in the eye now if he tried.

"Never let 'em take in your eyes," his father had drilled into him. "Keep 'em movin', or they'll know you and remember."

His father had been a shiftless sharecropper in Georgia, hardly any better'n a black slave, and they'd moved about from time to time, whenever his daddy got fed up with his luck and started blamin' the blacks or the overseer or the man in the big house.

There was always somethin' wrong. The seed was planted too late, the weeds grew too fast, the boll weevil come in too strong, the pickin' held off too long. It seemed as if his father had been given a ticket through life marked poverty, and he was so mad about it he was damned if he'd try to change it even if he could.

What he did was burn a barn or a haystack just as they were leavin' for the next county.

And every year it was harder to find a shack and a piece of ground.

Roark Shado had grown up watching his grim father sour. His sisters and brothers lit out young, since the old man would take a leather trace to them on any excuse because he was so damned mad at the world and his lot in it.

His mother had a new baby every year for nine years, and then she took sick, and it was all she could do to keep them all fed and no time at all for tenderness or learning or anything besides grubbing. Roark Shado had been eleven when she died—a mercy, he thought. He'd left a few months later after a hard fight with his father, which he'd lost, and he'd resolved never to lose another one.

He'd slipped away in the night, his back welted from the leather trace, a sore jaw and a black eye his patrimony.

He'd drifted, stealing and begging his food, to the riverboats, where he had an education in staying alive. No grand old man came along to pat him on the head and offer him a chance to learn the business. No sweet lady came along and offered him a scholarship to the University of Virginia.

No one came along and said, "You look hungry, son, here's a dollar, go have a good meal."

No one came along and said, "All you need to look like a sharp lad is a new suit of clothes and a pair of yellow boots."

No one said anything except "Git!"

In a way, his course had followed his father's. What he wanted, no one would give him, even though they had so much they could have shared out easily. He'd have worked, if he'd had a place to start, but on the docks there was nothing for a skinny boy.

The difference between himself and his father was that he didn't let the system turn him sour. He kept trying to come up out of his level any way he could. If he needed to lie, he lied. If he needed to steal, he stole. If he needed to trick or trap a rube, he learned how to do it.

By the time he was sixteen he had the yellow boots and halfway decent clothes because he had discovered that his greatest assets were his big brown eyes, which couldn't look a man in the eye, but which he could make as appealing as a puppy dog's when it came to gazing into a woman's face.

Once he learned how to make those brown eyes shine with ardor or longing he was well along in his profession. His only problem after that was to raise the level of his social position. The girls whose earnings he persuaded them to share were almost as poor as he was, and they sold their bodies cheaply.

Yet he knew there was another stratum of society where the same woman in a fancier dress and style could command a hundred times more than she could on the waterfront.

He might have continued well enough in his profession if the war had not come along and created unimaginable opportunities.

The south had to sell its cotton, and it had to import arms, and here was a young river rat who knew every device of corruption in the shipping business.

Early on, he realized people were looking at him as if he were a healthy enough specimen to join up and fight. For that reason he bought a cane and affected a slight limp. After a year of the war there were a lot of cripples coming back, and he assumed the role of a wounded veteran now working as an import-export broker.

Shiploads of cotton disappeared from the docks, and cases of odd-caliber, obsolete weapons arrived from all over Europe and commanded prices double and triple their value.

Young Shado considered himself a rich man on his twenty-first birthday. He had given up the procuring of women and made a fortune profiteering, but in his youthful enthusiasm he had not reckoned the war would end, nor that his Confederate greenbacks would turn out to be worthless.

So it was as the war ground down that this fortune disappeared and his business was finished. Worse, because the people were angry and looking for someone to blame for their defeat, the profiteers became their number one target.

Some were tarred and feathered. Some were shot in the night and thrown in the river. The shrewd ones, including Roark Shado, headed west without delay.

He only just escaped from the mob by stealing a horse and leaving everything behind. Traveling light, he managed to make his way to Texas, where, in the hardscrabble frontier country, he wasn't known and could start over again.

By the time he was twenty-one years old he'd seen the total bank of human corruption. He'd seen hundreds of valiant young men dying of the bloody flux and cholera, boys who wanted nothing more than to shoot a Yankee. He'd seen the profiteers and speculators. He'd seen boatloads of the maimed and wounded left over from battles that made no sense. He'd seen the rich south bled white and become a wasteland of powerless windbags, and he'd seen the belles of the plantations on the streets.

And he was glad, because now there was no one in the south who could say he or she was better than he. They were all mortal, corrupt pimps and harlots behind the pretense of romance and manners. In his mind there were no ladies nor gentlemen in the world and never had been. What he had seen was a foppery and dandyism and playacting made possible by the free labor of the slaves.

He wasn't an abolitionist or a reformer. He believed that the world was rotten and that anyone who thought otherwise deserved just what he got.

He despised them all for their hypocrisy.

The war had taught him that the strong were not merciful, the strong were not Christers, the strong were not do-gooders; the strong were completely ruthless and capable of any foul deed to achieve victory.

In that way he could cast his big brown eyes on the lady beside him at the table and suggest it was time she went upstairs and got to work.

The lady nodded and asked, "Will you come up later, Rory?"

"I'll try, Lorena," he lied, his limpid eyes gazing soulfully into hers in spite of the contempt he felt.

They were all hypocrites, just as much as the men, he'd discovered. Rarely had he found a woman of genuine passion willing to sell it. Most of them pretended the passion and were cold and indifferent in lovemaking; but, moaning and breathing hard, they sold their pretense and enjoyed a sense of revenge in the selling of a false product and the controlling of the transaction.

They were no better than he, and they were stupid besides. At least he knew the whole gamut of rottenness and wasn't afraid of it. He sometimes thought that mankind's corruption was his best friend.

He looked upon his use of the network of houses as a part of his brokerage business, in which, as in any other business, you buy low and sell high.

Now, staring at the backs of the three big men, he saw them as he saw everyone else—as liars and cheats working on some scheme to interfere in his business and steal his property.

If they cluttered their minds with idealism or charity or altruism or honor or justice, it was all the worse for them, because he had no words like that in his mind to hinder the execution of his plans.

The youngest of that threesome bothered him most. He was big and tough as a bulldogger, but worse, he had an electric hatred sparking in his eyes for no reason Roark Shado could fathom from his past.

"Who's the cowboy in the cowhide vest?" Roark Shado asked Potter quietly.

Potter shot a glance at the doorway and replied, "Name's Isham Rye, if that means anything."

"Not to me. You think he's for real?"

"Who knows around here? There's no way of checking." Potter shrugged his shoulders. "They seemed to believe my yarn about the new army."

"Why not? It's not a bad idea."

"That's it, an idea, a chick ready to hatch."

"That fat man looks familiar," Rainy Day said, cutting the deck of cards over and over. "He's from Texas. Maybe El Paso or San Antone, I don't recall."

"He said he was from Fort Worth, representing some investors in the cattle business."

"Could be true," Shado said. "There's eastern money and even some milords from England wanting to cash in on the free grass."

The marshal came in and looked over the tables until he noticed Shado beckoning to him.

Taking a chair, he asked, "What can I do for you?"

"Keep an eye on those three strangers that came in this morning. They don't seem too anxious to leave."

"I know who you mean. The young one got the best of Patch."

"I judged he could because Patch won't use his

brains," Shado said, lighting a cheroot. "That cowboy has been around some."

"Why don't I just shoot him if he's goin' to be a problem?" Day muttered.

"I'm not saying no, I'm just saying take your time. I'd like to know what they're up to first."

"Whatever's right," Rainy Day said indifferently. "I'll curl him up whenever you say."

"Don't be over confident, Rainy," the marshal said. "The other one swamped Virgil."

"Hell, Virgil wasn't fast," Day snorted. "He'd only fight a dude."

"And he made a mistake."

"That old guy is no dude. He just looks like one," Shado said.

"Do I lead 'em on with the army and the New South, or do I just try to see their money?" Potter asked nervously. Talk of guns and gunfighting gave him dyspepsia.

"Play it slow, a day at a time. We're here, they got to make their play. Then we look at what there is in it for us."

"You're a cool one, Mr. Shado." Day looked up from his solitaire. "Always playin' it safe."

"The dealer calls his own game." Shado smiled. "And I'm dealer in Blood Cut."

Shado was thinking about the new Confederate Army. It wasn't a bad idea at all, except that the Union Army was about finished fighting Indians and wouldn't take to the idea of somebody starting a new country right in the middle of the road. Brigham Young could get away with it for a while because he picked a spot so god-awful far away, no one would bother him until he got too big for his britches.

Killing all them women and children up at Mountain Meadow was too big a massacre to hush up, and it wouldn't be long before old Brigham swung for it. At least he should, but justice being blind, he might wiggle out of it and put the blame on somebody else.

No, he wasn't about to take on the U.S. Army. If Lee and Jackson and Beauregard and Hood couldn't beat 'em, Roark Shado wasn't about to try.

Going to have to make a move on Nan Packard pretty soon, he thought. Don't want to scare her off, though. Women like to think they were holding all the cards, and you let 'em go on thinking that while you switch the decks. Next thing they know is they're low, contemptible animals good for only one thing, and that is to please a man. Nan Packard thought she was so independent and so pretty and smart and even range tough, but he'd known twenty or thirty others just as proud before he'd humbled them.

It was a slow game, but he enjoyed it because he always won.

Yellow-haired Nan, so fresh and saucy, was next in line.

He might even get a fake preacher like Deacon Trotter in the game and deal her the Ace of Matrimony. Take a honeymoon to New Orleans and put her to work.

"What are you thinkin' on?" Rainy Day dared to ask.

"Why?" Roark Shado replied coldly.

"You had a smile on your face like a coyote finding a nest of bunny rabbits. I just wondered."

"I was thinking I might have to go to New Orleans on business before winter."

Suddenly Rainy Day's face changed as he looked over Roark Shado's shoulder and saw the woman with the small two-shooter. He could have drawn and killed her because the derringer was aimed at Shado's back, but he knew he'd hang for it. No one in the west shot women, even if they were sporters. It was an ironclad custom that you could beat a woman or whip her, you could take off her shoes and kick her out in a blizzard, but one thing you couldn't do was kill her.

Potter looked to his right and saw her coming. He skidded his chair back quickly out of the line of fire.

"You got a problem with Sally, boss," Day said through his teeth, his lips not moving.

Alertly, Roark Shado rose and turned slightly, lifting his hands so that he was obviously unprepared to fight, but also in a posture of welcome.

"Come sit down, sweetheart, I've been longin' to see you."

"Don't give me no more of your snake oil, Rory. I'm fed up to my back teeth with it."

"Now, Sally, sit down. What would you like to drink?"

Sally held the two-bore with both hands to keep it steadily aimed at Shado's breastbone.

Completely calm, he sat back in the chair and said, "Tell me your troubles, Sally. I haven't any idea of what's goin' on."

Sally might have been a big-busted beauty in her brief youth, but now she was hardened, her hair dyed jet black, her eyes encircled by mascara, the hard lines in her face buried in makeup.

"I'll tell you, Rory. Lorena came up and said you told her she was number one. Now you better listen to me, Rory. I done a lot for you, and you can't treat me this way."

"Of course not, Sally, love. Put down that pistol before you cause a terrible accident. I want to tell you of our new plans."

"What new plans?" She glared at him suspiciously.

"I'm not so sure now," he replied doubtfully. "I thought you cared about me, I thought we had a future together, but now . . ."

"You promised we'd buy a resort back east for rich

people with our money. Now you're sending up Lorena and settin' me down."

"We're goin' to do it, but we need Lorena's help, too. We're all workin' for the same thing. Don't you understand?" he asked persuasively in his soft southern drawl. "Another year and I think we can do it."

Still holding the pistol in both hands, she settled down in the chair just vacated by Everett Potter.

"Why don't you just tell me the truth, and I won't shoot you."

"I'm tellin' you the truth and nothin' but the truth, so help me God." He placed his hand over his heart. "One more year and we'll quit the circus and start livin' like the swells."

Rainy Day was disgusted to be involved in the scene. He didn't think it was manly or proper to listen to a sporter threatening a man.

Still, it wasn't his business, thank God. He liked to face a man, any man, and shoot 'im down, and he didn't like the dry stock.

He saw the stout Madame Lily making a slow circle through the silent men in the room, coming their way.

"Want me to leave?" he asked Shado.

"Stay still," Roark Shado said coldly. "Sally and I aren't ashamed of anything."

"That's right!" She turned her anger on Rainy Day, laying the small pistol on the table. "You ain't so pure you can't stand hearing people talkin' out their troubles."

Lily came up alongside Sally and put a friendly hand on her shoulder. "Feelin' better, dearie?"

"I guess so. It's just I get so lonesome when Rory don't come talk to me."

"I've been very busy, Sally, but I'll make it up to you," Shado replied, his big brown eyes misting.

"Now don't feel bad, Rory. I know you're doin' your best. We'll pull through, don't you ever doubt it."

"Sometimes I hardly have the heart to go on," he murmured.

"Now, now, baby, one more year and we'll have us a fancy spa in Saratoga or someplace."

"Maybe we ought to get out of here. Go somewhere else for a fresh start."

"Where'd you like to go?" Sally asked.

"I been thinkin' about winterin' in Havana. Lots of swells goin' there from New York for a good time. We could make some real money over there."

"Whatever you say, love." Sally seemed ready to go to sleep, all her adrenaline used up.

"You look tired, sweetheart," Shado said. "Lily, why don't you take Sally upstairs and let her rest before we go?"

"Where'd you say we're goin', sweetie?" Sally asked, her eyes blank.

"Havana, Cuba, honey. Get your clothes packed."

"C'mon, Sal," Lily said, and she escorted the confused Sally away while Roark Shado pocketed the small gun.

"You goin' to Cuba, boss?" Rainy Day asked, amazement in his voice."

"Not me. Sal's goin' to Cuba. I have a business associate there who will take good care of her." Roark Shado let a little smile play over his thin lips.

10

Killing Roark Shado wouldn't be an easy thing. Shado always kept a screen of men loosely gathered about and could fade away behind their protection, leaving Isham Rye to be cut down by his gunfighters before he could accomplish anything.

With that in mind, he decided Nan Packard deserved a warning before anything else.

The liveryman had advised him about the crusty old brothers who didn't take to strangers coming onto their land, but Isham rode in confidence. So long as he didn't sneak around, he didn't think the brothers would bother him overmuch.

Besides, he needed a ride in the good clean air to settle down. In town he'd been ready to fight the Shado cohorts barehanded and might have lost it right then if Julius hadn't cooled his rage with a soft voice and fatherly wisdom.

Hard to believe he was a U.S. marshal. Those marshals weren't political hacks, they were all men. You couldn't survive any other way on the frontier.

The Nebraska soil was deep and rich, but it wasn't

any better than his own land near San Juan Bautista, and there it never snowed or hailed, never was a winter-kill blizzard nor a rampaging flood in the Pajaro River. Most times it was warm, but with a breeze in the afternoon coming off the Pacific Ocean and blowing through Chittenden Pass down across the valley.

San Francisco was only a day's ride to the north, and you didn't have to worry about being scalped by wild Indians on the way. In the year he'd been there building his house and barn he'd come to understand just how hard the living was on the windswept plains.

Still, for those coming from arid Texas or hardscrabble hills of Tennessee, it was a paradise needing only a plough and a lot of sweat.

The San Juan Bautista ranch was just one step onward in richness and comfort.

Sooner or later he'd find a woman to match the land, but he wasn't hunting a wife. He wanted the house to be finished and the range stocked before he started a family. Not that he wanted his children to be born in luxury and grow up as false aristocrats. No, he wanted a family so close to the land there was no worker or caretaker in between. It was the only way they could really understand their living, something that had taken a war and the misery afterward for him to learn the hard way.

Reaching the picket fence and the closed gate, he looked first for someone working outside, and failing that, he called, "Hello the house!"

An old man carrying a shotgun emerged from the front door.

"What do you want?"

"I'm peaceable. I don't want nothin' except to parley with the Packard family."

"I'm Packard. Speak your piece."

"Is your daughter home?"

"What you want with her?"

"She's a part of my parley."

"You barkin' up the wrong tree, mister. She's already spoken for."

Isham put a curb on his temper as his anger at the stubborn, inhospitable old coot rose.

"That's what I want to talk about."

"You ought to be talkin' to Roark Shado," the old man shouted, "if you was any kind of a man at all."

"I aim to kill that man as soon as I leave here," Isham responded.

The door opened, and yellow-haired, freckled Nan appeared.

"What is it, Daddy?"

"Man wants to talk about Mister Shado."

"Light down and come in." She came to the fence and opened the gate.

Dismounting, he tethered the claybank and walked to the porch with her, the hunch-shouldered old man watching him like an eagle.

"That's far enough."

"Oh, Daddy," she said lightly, sizing up the big rancher as if appraising his value to her.

Isham noticed she wore a low-cut blouse and that her breasts were young and firm, and he'd known enough women to realize that she'd only put that blouse on a moment ago to test her femininity on him. He wasn't impressed. He reflected that maybe he'd been weaned too long ago.

Her wide face seemed open and innocent, especially with the freckles dotting her nose, but her eyes were busy scouring about, weighing and evaluating, passing the information back to a calculating brain.

What she saw was a man big enough and strong enough to suit her needs, but his clothing, though serviceable and of good quality, was worn, and he had no gold watch chain or diamond jewelry, while his hair looked as if a logger had cut it a long time ago.

So she didn't instantly exclude him as a possible mate, but she put him down the list below Roark Shado and above the kid, Tony Barr.

"Got me all classed and pegged?" he asked.

She blushed, and her eyes fired.

"Just say your piece, mister."

"My piece starts back down in Louisiana," he said tiredly, not wanting to lay his guts out anymore. Still, he had to give warning. If the girl closed her ears to it, it was her business. His duty as a human being was to give her a choice she didn't know she had.

"Yes," she prompted him matter-of-factly, "Louisiana."

"Was a couple sisters lived next to us. Me'n the older one was good friends, but we lost track of each other in the war. They moved to Texas, and I tried makin' a livin' farther west, never knowin' where they were. Then I sold out and went to California."

"Looking for gold?" she asked.

"No, lookin' for a peaceable ranch where I'd never have to shoot anybody again."

"Did you find it?"

"Yes, ma'am, but that isn't my piece."

"Go ahead then."

"I got a letter out there that'd been passed from here to there and back again and took over a year to reach me. Said her sister was in trouble and needed help."

"So like a knight on a white horse you rode back to Texas to defend the fair maiden," she said, giggling.

"I was raised believin' it is a duty to stand by old friends." He flushed. "I'll cut this short."

"Please do," she said. "I have a feeling I know what you're going to say."

"The older sister was murdered in El Paso before I

ever got there. The younger sister had gone off to New Orleans with a man described as a southern gentleman."

"So?"

"He wasn't a southern gentleman."

"How could you know?"

"He wore yellow boots."

The prankish, scheming face froze as the message hit her.

"You are talking about my fiancé?"

"I'd hoped it hadn't gone that far."

"Suppose it's true," she said testily, squaring her shoulders. "He's a mature man. I'd expect him to have known a few women."

"Ma'am, he not only knows them, he sells them," Isham said softly.

"You lie!" Quick as a cat she slapped his face with her open right hand.

Isham didn't back up.

"Why aren't you telling this to him, you coward?" she exploded. "Running around behind an honorable man's back talking dirty!"

"I'm goin' to try to kill him today, but I figured in case him or his gang happened to stop me, at least you'd know the truth."

"Of course you have no evidence."

"Both my friends are dead."

"It happens," Nan said, "that Mr. Shado saved me from just such a life not too long ago. He faced up to that man Patch and that gunfighter Day and brought me safely home. He made no improper advances and asked no favors for his gallantry. Now get out!"

"You heard her." Old Packard waved the ten-gauge at Isham.

"I'll stick that goose gun up your nose, you point it at me again!" Isham was angry at himself, the old man, the girl, Shado, and the whole dim-damned shebang.

"I done told you, girl," he said. He turned his back to the pair and walked to the gate.

"We don't mean to be unfriendly," the girl called, still trying to keep all her avenues open.

He said nothing. Mounting up, he touched his hat and rode back the way he'd come.

"He'll kill you!" she yelled after him, but he wasn't listening.

11

'Bout time we aimed south for Coleman County, John."

The tall cowboy named Ansom poured the last grains of tobacco from the bag into the folded paper.

"It's a week to payday, Anse," John said, "and if that feller Rainy Day don't bring us some grub, we're goin' to have to boil our boots."

They were sitting by their small campfire watching their jackrabbit stew bubble in its iron pot.

"Payday, we aim for Texas, John. I want to be home before winter."

"You mean you ain't goin' to take a run at them pretty females in Blood Cut first?"

"These critters is some worry to me. We drawin' down top hand wages, but we could be hung for rustlin' cows that ain't ours and never will be."

"Rainy said he'd watch our back trail. I just doubt anybody'll get by him."

"But as I see it, we ought to have a share. Say fifty-fifty."

"You mean three hundred for Rainy and three hundred for us?"

"Fact is, John, I was thinkin' on three hundred for you and three hundred for me."

"That'd be some chancy."

"We're in it now. We done all the work and took all the risks, and we ain't been shot or hanged yet. Why not just keep right on with it?"

The punchers were camped at the entrance of a small valley deep in spring grass. The herd of rustled steers were satisfied to stay there and make tallow and were disinclined to move out.

They still wore the Block Diamond brand and the right ear over split.

"Where on earth could we sell critters so marked up?" John asked.

"Supposin' we just drove 'em west to Denver. Nobody out there'd know the difference."

"Well, my daddy always said cows belong to the man who can sell 'em." John chuckled.

"That feller Rainy'd be some salty."

"You got any better ideas, Ansom?"

"I got holes in my boots, and my hat's attractin' grease eaters," Ansom drawled. "When do we start?"

"We can't leave till Rainy Day brings us some grub. Today or tomorrow."

"Then soon as he rides back to Blood Cut we head 'em up west. It'll be a week before he comes back, and we'll be long gone by then."

"Make a tidy little stake to winter on."

John cocked his ear and faced the prairie.

"Someone comin'."

"One horse."

"Speakin' of the devil, it must be the boss. I hope he brought plenty of the makin's."

They stood waiting until the rider came over a low

hill, and they could see he was alone and riding a pinto horse.

"That ain't Day, damn it," Ansom growled.

"It's that damn dude kid. What we goin' to tell him?"

"He don't know beans from buckshot, so we just tell him we're herdin' our cattle."

Seeing the punchers and the camp, Tony Barr slowed the pinto to an easy walk as he approached.

He had no definite plan except to escape from Sam Diggs. After that he could think on Nan Packard and her father and that smooth slicker named Shado. After he had them all settled in his mind he could think of his father and the family.

That was enough thinking for anybody.

He was tired and hungry and mad besides.

Everyone treated him as if he were a dumb kid just because he hadn't been born on horseback with a six-gun in one hand and a lasso in the other.

They didn't know there was a whole different world back east. Trolleys and police in uniform. Universities . . .

Suppose one of these bowlegged, tall-hatted waddies walked into the Harvard Quad and started twirling his six-shooter. Why, they'd lock him up in the zoo!

Suppose you started talking about Immanuel Kant and Schopenhauer and philosophies to one of these supermen. He'd think you were talking Chinese.

Suppose you gave him a salad for lunch!

What would he think if he ever saw himself in a full-length mirror? He'd run!

Suppose you asked him to play badminton or squash, or to scull down the river.

Suppose you took him to the gymnasium and invited him to a match of Greco-Roman wrestling.

No, no, there's nothing wrong with me, he thought.

It's the irresponsible westerners that think they're so almighty superior.

What rankled him most was the way Nan had shunted him aside when he needed her loyalty most. He couldn't understand that. Someone had once told him women lived by their own rules that no man had ever figured out, and he blamed his predicament on that; but beautiful Nan was so exceptional, she should have seen how false that Shado was and how right he was. Still, she'd been pressured by her father.

It was only proper that she should accede to paternal authority, but she should have learned how to temper that authority and inject intelligence into it.

His mother never argued with his father, yet she lived exactly as she wished to live—never, of course, overstepping the boundaries of proper society.

He saw the two cowboys standing by their fire, and, smelling the delicious aroma of simmering stew, he rode close. He'd already learned that it was improper to dismount before receiving permission, and he waited politely. Over the cowboys' heads he could see the small herd of beeves grazing belly-deep in grass.

He assumed there would be a ranch house nearby.

"Afternoon," Ansom said. "Light and set."

"Thank you," Tony replied, and he dismounted. "Nice-looking bunch of cattle."

"They'll do," John said. "You're a long way out of Blood Cut on your own."

"Just looking over the country. Would you happen to need an extra hand driving the cattle?"

"No, reckon not," Ansom said. "Let's eat."

"Is the ranch nearby?" Tony asked, filling his mess kit with stew.

"If they was a ranch close by, we wouldn't be eatin' rabbit stew without biscuits," John said, gnawing at a leg bone.

"How long have you been out here?" Tony asked, trying to make polite dinner conversation.

"Not long," Ansom said.

"Long enough," John said, wishing the kid would just shut up, eat, and get out.

Ansom glumly decided it was already too late. The kid had seen the cattle; all he had to do was start blabbing to the first person he met. They'd lose the whole shebang and likely get strung up besides.

Damn the luck!

"What do you plan to do with the cattle?" Tony asked innocently.

"Watch 'em," John said.

"You mean guard them from rustlers?"

"Reckon so." John smiled.

"What outfit do you work for?"

"Block Diamond," Ansom said, thinking it was a brilliant reply.

"I've heard of it." Tony nodded wisely. "The boss came into camp looking—"

"What was he lookin' for, kid?" John asked, putting his bowl carefully off to one side and climbing to his feet.

Tony flushed as he realized what he'd said, and that these were the rustled cattle.

"He said he was looking for some extra hands." Tony tried to cover up.

"That so?" Ansom commented, his eyes leveled on the kid.

"Yes. I offered, but he said I was too young," Tony stammered. "Thank you for the stew. I guess I'll be riding on."

"Set a while longer," Ansom said. "We don't get many visitors."

"That's a fact," John agreed, waiting for Ansom to take the lead.

"I guess my friends will start looking for me if I'm

late," Tony said, backing up, knowing full well he could outrun the two punchers, but he couldn't catch and mount the pinto before they'd have him.

"Funny how an easterner makes so many friends," Tony said.

"What friends are you talking about, youngster?" Ansom asked.

"The Packards—Walter Packard and his daughter. They'll be expecting me."

"They live way upriver," John said doubtfully.

"But we're supposed to meet for dinner in Blood Cut." Tony tried desperately to lie his way out, but he knew he'd already made the cardinal blunder, and they were only playing with him now.

"Too bad you gon' disappoint 'em," Ansom said.

"I'm going," Tony said, and he turned toward the pinto.

He heard three clicks of a single-action Colt hammer being drawn back to full cock. A touch of the trigger and he'd be dead.

Turning back, he forced a smile. "No need for that."

Ansom's big thumb held the hammer back as he pulled the trigger, then let the hammer gently back down.

"Glad you think so. Maybe we can work somethin' out," John said.

"For sure, you're goin' first," Ansom said to Tony.

"Well, let's discuss the matter intelligently," Tony declared. "You have the six hundred head of Block Diamond steers, and I wish I hadn't dropped by to discover them, but I have, and there's no way around that."

"That is exactly a bull's-eye." Ansom nodded.

"But if I promise faithfully to never say a word about you or these cattle, could you not accept my word as my bond?"

"No," John said.

"We'd have no way of collectin'," Ansom said.

"Very well, then take me in. I'll share the guilt."

"Can't," John said.

"Why not? I don't even want a share of the money."

"That ain't it," Ansom said. "We're goin' to have to tie you up off down by the creek until the boss comes and tells us what to do."

"Oh," Tony said dispiritedly, "I didn't realize there were others involved."

"So it is. Otherwise we could use you, but it ain't our say-so now," Ansom explained apologetically.

"C'mon, youngster," John said, digging out some leather piggin' strings from his saddlebag. "Don't give me any trouble, you ain't dead yet."

They took him and the pinto down into a little draw where there was a small sand bank and tied his hands behind his back, hobbled his legs, and picketed the pinto close by.

"I'm goin' tell you, son, I want to pull you out of this, but if the boss finds out you're here, I can't save you."

"So if you want to keep livin', you better keep quiet," John finished for him.

Back in camp they tried to erase the pinto's tracks and any sign Tony might have left.

"Why don't we just turn him over to Rainy Day?" John asked, tired of so many problems in one day.

"'Cause we need another hand to ride drag when we move them cows west."

"You mean you'd take him in?"

"Why not? He said he wanted to join up without pay. We'd go a lot faster with a third hand."

"But suppose he talks."

"We leave him at Denver. If he talks, he gets hung. We won't be waitin' around."

"But if Rainy Day gets wise—"

"That's the touchy part. We're goin' to have to work up a good story just in case he does."

"There's plenty of time." John smiled. It seemed like everything was coming up bluebonnets from cow chips. "I never had a run of luck this good before."

"That's what worries me," Ansom said. "When I'm off my home range I'm all gurgle and no guts."

Rainy Day had never been much of a rider or a lover of fresh air. The pallor on his skull-like face was proof enough of his preference for the inside of a saloon, the smokier the better. He'd worked his way up from saloon chore boy to bartender, and in that capacity he had been put in the position of having to kill a couple of cantankerous, bullheaded customers too drunk to hit the spittoon with their hats.

After that no one wanted to buy a drink from him, and he took to gambling and making small undercover deals that made him an adequate living with a minimum amount of work.

The gambling kept getting him into trouble because he was a poor cheater. A poor cheater has to shoot quicker, and he became known as a top gun soon enough. Since no one would play cards with him, he moved into the killing business.

Sometimes it was as simple as hearing about an old man hoarding gold pieces. You go out to his ranch, catch him alone, start cutting his fingers off, dig out the gold, and then kill him. Other times it'd be bounty hunting. And other times he could be hired by a weaker man to pick a fight with a stronger man.

It wasn't as simple as selling shoes, but it paid well enough, and it wasn't outside work where you got your hands dirty.

He wished they hadn't pegged that "Rainy" on him. He'd have preferred being called the Doctor. Here comes Doc Day ready to operate with his .45. Doctor Death. No, Doctor Day sounded good enough.

Roark Shado had heard of his reputation and hunted him down while he was resting in Matamoros after an unsavory fracas, and he sketched out his future if he'd come into the organization. He explained there were wine, women, and song in Blood Cut, and it didn't need saying that Matamoros was fat and dead.

There was an unlimited future in Blood Cut if he played it right, and there was nothing to lose in going.

"You act like you're boss, and that gives me the cover to move around and listen. I'll be the southern gentleman looking for a ranch."

"Is that all?" Rainy had asked.

"We'll have a marshal, but you'll have the gun. You're the enforcer, so you take care of anybody crossing you. You play it like it's your town."

He'd liked that part of it. Hardly anyone wanted to cross him. This far north there weren't a bunch of fumbling kid gunfighters looking for hash marks. It was plumb peaceable, and Shado had been right. There was plenty to drink, and plenty of women to drink with. Maybe André Brown wasn't exactly the world's best brass band, but at least he could make a tune out of the squeeze box.

Things had been going along right well. More and more wagon trains coming through to pay their toll, and more business springing up, but then Shado had the idea of rustling those Block Diamond cows.

"Easy money," he'd said.

Easy for him after he'd recruited the punchers to do the work, but now he was pushing it off on him. "Take a sack of grub out to the boys," he'd said. "Show 'em you can hit a crow in the ass with one shot." Rainy Day hadn't any choice.

"Alone?"

"Take Zinc. He's getting saddle sores from riding the bar stool."

He and Zinc had gone down to the Mercantile and charged a side of bacon, a sack of cornmeal, a bucket of lard, and some airtights of tomatoes and peaches.

"Whiskey? Tobacco?" Zinc asked, his muddy eyes looking down. Rainy Day liked Zinc to keep his eyes down because he thought half-breeds damn well ought to keep their eyes down.

"The hell with 'em," Rainy said. "Let's ride."

He hadn't seen the sun in a month, and he pulled his hat brim down over his eyes.

Why the hell did Shado send him when any dim-witted hand could do the same thing?

Of course. It was shootin' the crow in the ass that was his real purpose, even if there wasn't no crows. You let two drifters handle a bunch of mavericks that nobody owns, pretty soon they think they own 'em, and off they go.

But you give 'em a hard eye, do some trick shootin', and that'll hold 'em quiet for a spell.

The trouble was you couldn't just shoot 'em, otherwise you'd have nobody guarding the herd.

Damn, he hadn't shot anybody for a week of Sundays. Getting soft. Have to watch it. Just setting around playing solitaire and breaking in the new girls wasn't improving the skill he lived by.

A man needs to keep sharp, he thought, needs to face an up-and-coming youngster once in a while. You stay out of the game, they start thinking you can't roll and draw, begin to think you don't care to play the game anymore.

The breed, Zinc, rode along beside him with the grub tied in a gunny sack behind his saddle.

"What do you think, Zinc?" Rainy thought it was funny rhyming think with Zinc.

"Me?"

"I ain't talkin' to your horse. Think Zinc?"

"What's there to think? I pass a day at a time."

"That all?"

"We live, we die," the half-breed said.

Rainy thought he could easily turn that remark into reason for a fight. He'd kill the breed faster'n chain lightning with a link snapped.

As he shifted in his saddle Zinc said, "No offense, Mr. Day."

What the hell could you do with such a humble, abject bastard? Ought to drop him just for that, he thought.

But then who'd you have to talk to?

"You know where we're goin'?"

"Yes, sir," Zinc said, knowing death rode next to him.

"We want to scare the pie waddin' out of them two dumb Texans. You know why?"

"So they won't steal the herd."

"Right." Rainy nodded. "Remember to stay in front of me, and remember I'm behind you."

"You don't trust me, boss?" Zinc asked.

"I don't trust anybody. You or them, or God or the devil."

"It's hard."

"Happens I like it that way," Rainy said, and suddenly he stabbed his hand low, palmed the .45, lifted, and sighted in a scampering prairie dog, but he didn't fire.

"You soft on prairie dogs?" Zinc murmured.

"I ain't soft on prairie dogs or anything on two legs," Rainy said. "Happens I don't want to announce our comin'."

"Just wonderin'," the breed said.

Twirling the six-shooter, Rainy tossed it to his left

hand in the border shift, twirled it once, caught it in his right hand again, and neatly returned it to its holster.

"By God, that feels so good, I'm goin' to have to blow out somebody's lamp just to top it off," Rainy Day said, grinning.

12

Sam Diggs had been moseying around in the voluminous back of the Mercantile, inspecting the pharmaceuticals, thinking a little tonic might lift his spirits and possibly rejuvenate what he was coming to believe was a hopelessly ruined body.

Studying the shelves while Olaf Hundertmarx was cutting meat for a customer in the front of the store, he read the fanciful labels: King's Discovery, Swift's Specific, Ayer's Ague Cure, Rheumatic Syrup, Kennedy Discovery, Pierce Prescription, Scott's Emulsion, Golden Medical Discovery, Martin's Panacea, Cuticura Resolvent, Vigor of Life, Coe's Balsam, Nervine, B.B. Cordial, Wizard Oil, Tincture of Rhubarb, Zinc Lobelia, Sweet Nitre, Cremoline . . . enough panaceas and rejuvenators to make a man's mind numb.

Hundertmarx's daughter, Greta, came trotting back to the counter, her round body squared off somewhat by a harness of whalebones and lacings, her bosom thereby uplifted like a sideboard holding melons.

"Can I get you something?" she asked with a heavy Teutonic accent.

Sam had meant to try a bottle of the Vigor of Life, but he couldn't bring himself to mention such a thing to a lady.

"I'm just studyin' the bottles, ma'am."

"No aches or pains?" She chuckled. "Maybe you need a little lifter-upper, *ja?*"

"No, ma'am, I'm strong as a bull."

"Ah!" Her blue eyes teased him.

"I mean—I'm feelin' like most men comin' on forty feel."

"Then maybe a bottle of Chamberlain's Oyster Extract would fix you right up. What I mean is, sometimes a man, as strong as a bull even, needs a little helper-outer once in a while." She touched his battered hand with the tips of her pale white fingers.

Sam blushed and wondered if the sweat showed on his forehead.

"To tell the truth, ma'am, I was wonderin' if you had somethin' for a toothache."

"Oh, sure," she said, disappointed, her smile fading. "We got Graffenburg's Toothache Drops right here for only ten cents a bottle. How many toothaches you got?"

"One, ma'am, just one," Sam said, digging a dime out of his pocket and accepting the little bottle wrapped in a twist of newspaper.

"You need anything else, big fella," she murmured, "you just let me know."

"Yes'm, I will," Sam Diggs replied cautiously, and he turned away, humbled all the more.

From the front of the store he heard the disagreeable nasal tones of Rainy Day ordering from a list. "Ten pounds of cornmeal, side of bacon, bucket of lard . . ."

He stepped back in the shadows of the children's department to examine the rocking horses on the counter. Brightly painted steeds awaiting a lucky child's Christmas in this remote hamlet, they stared at him with impudent eyes. He touched a rocker with his finger to set it bobbing back and forth quietly like a clock's pendulum.

"Put it on Shado's bill."

"Yes, sir, Mr. Day."

"And don't pad it out none either."

"*Ach, nein, nein,* I never do such a thing ever."

Hundertmarx seemed to be near tears in his defense.

Methinks he protests too much, Sam thought, smiling as Rainy Day and his companion, a swarthy man wearing a greasy, battered hat with an eagle feather tucked into the band, went out the door.

"What devilment you suppose he's up to now?" he asked the rocking horse. "Think I ought to follow him?"

The rocking horse solemnly nodded.

Sam drifted slowly toward the front door and bought a sack of lemon snaps from old man Hundertmarx, giving Day time to set his packs and ride out.

He didn't need to keep them in sight. Their fresh tracks were easily visible in the soft earth and went in a straight line without any traps or ruses complicating the trail.

Munching on the cookies, Sam wondered if perhaps the pair ahead of him was going to California. That would be about his luck.

He was following a blind hunch mainly because it was all he had. He might have asked Isham or Julius to come along, but why bother them for what would probably turn out to be another wild-goose chase?

No doubt they'd do just as well following their own leads.

Once clear of Blood Cut the tracks stretched out, and Sam lifted the bay into a mile-eating canter to match.

The green prairie stretched out ahead of him like a limitless sward of grass broken only by patches of bluebonnets or buttercups, and a few undulating low hills and creeks that drained the great pasture.

What a fine country, Sam thought. Why couldn't the people be as fresh and true?

His second thought was that he'd been at his desk too long sitting in an oak swivel chair. He had to put more weight in the stirrups to ease his chafed and battered sitter.

Gradually the flatland yielded to low rolling hills as the trail turned northerly, and Sam had to slow the bay so as not to overrun his quarry accidentally.

What was a man his age doing out there riding after a pair of cutthroats? Why wasn't he back in St. Joe contemplating what he would have for supper at Delmonico's?

Simple enough. He needed the money.

Not only that, he resented being banged over the head by an antique potato head, and even more than that, he was beginning to understand that the kid had as much determination to resist returning to his father as Sam had to take him back.

A rack of buffalo bones, white against the green, jogged his vagrant thoughts, and instinctively he drew up to look again at the tracks. They should have some sort of a landmark to identify their destination. You couldn't just go out for a ride and expect to reach a certain ranch or cow camp without some sense of the whole country.

Yonder on a distant hillside he saw a ledge of

cream-colored limestone exposed on a hillside, and he sighted the tracks of the two horses on it. They aimed right for that prominent landmark. Sam held back, trying to decide to go either left or right, because for sure he didn't want to come right on top of a den of rattlesnakes.

He circled to the right for no reason at all and rode slowly, keeping below the rim of the hill until he came to a line of cottonwood trees paralleling a slough. There he used the cover to come around the slope, where he could see into the next little valley.

Why, in all this huge, empty pasture, should a herd of fat beeves be gathered right exactly here? There was no sign of ranch buildings or gathering corrals. Perhaps some immigrant pilgrim was driving the herd to the gold fields, hoping for extra profit.

Yet there had been no fresh wagon tracks nor sign of drovers, and he knew that if he went on around the hill he'd see the camp that Rainy and his sidekick had aimed for. Someone was guarding the herd, and that someone had to have supplies brought in.

Rainy Day had bought only a side of bacon and a few other staples, which meant to Sam that there was at least one puncher riding herd on these critters, but not more than three.

Then he saw the Block Diamond brand and added it up.

Dismounting and tethering the bay to a cottonwood log, Sam moved in a crouch on around the hill, using the grass and creekside brush for cover.

Higher up on the hillside he saw the little bench where the punchers had made camp out of the wind. There they could oversee the hidden valley where the cattle grazed and keep out of harm's way at the same time.

There were the horses, three of them, and the

waddies standing around a little fire. One of them was unloading supplies from the back of his horse.

He heard a dry twig snap behind him and, without thinking, quickly rolled to his left as a gun butt came crashing down where his head had been a moment before. Holding the six-gun by the barrel, a bull-shouldered cowboy came lunging forward, falling down the slope.

Sam scrambled down the hill to get his feet set, and as the heavy cowboy swung at his leg with the six-gun Sam kicked at the flailing arm and knocked the gun loose.

Why hadn't the idiot just shot him instead of trying to brain him, Sam wondered, but hardly had he framed the thought when the big cowboy leapt from his kneeling position and bulled Sam down into the dry creek bottom.

He doesn't want those others to hear us, flashed the thought just as a rock-hard fist smashed into his jaw, bouncing him against the bank.

Again he rolled aside to miss the charging cowboy, and he managed to clip him behind the ear as he went by.

Staggering to keep his balance, Sam caught the turning cowboy with his own right cross before the other could get set, but he took a counter left to his midriff that popped the air out of him and sent him falling backward into a tangle of ninebark vines.

As the cowboy came charging again Sam lifted both feet and drove the cowboy reeling backward.

But Sam was too tangled up in the vines to take advantage, and the cowboy bounced back with both fists swinging like mauls at a glut. Sam tasted blood in his mouth, and his brain seemed to start going around in lazy circles like a buzzard riding a thermal. Weakly he put his hands out to guard and clinch with his younger opponent until he could get his head clear, but the puncher wrestled loose and came across with another slugging right hand that brought gray twilight into Sam's brain.

With a last-ditch effort he swung his own right and felt it connect, but his world was going dark, and he thought he'd never know how it came out.

I'm too old to live, he thought.

As he slowly crumpled into the creek bottom he thought he heard a wet smacking sound and a heavy exhalation, but he couldn't stay around long enough to be sure. His mind resisted the inevitable conscious pounding banging between his ears, and he wondered why his boot heels were bouncing about, feeling curious about the surcingle under his arms and around his chest.

"C'mon, Sam." He heard an urgent whisper filtering through the labyrinthine cavern that was his head and thought, That's strange—and he slipped off again for a few moments. Then he felt someone slapping his face and remembered the urgent whisper, "C'mon, Sam."

Who? Who doin'—Who doin' what? Slappin', who doin' that?

"C'mon, Sam."

"Okay!" he said to stop the slapping.

"C'mon, Sam, we got to ride."

He recognized the kid's voice and thought how lucky he was to have caught him once again, and then he considered that maybe it was the other way. He had been caught by the kid.

But then who was he fighting down there in that cursed draw?

A cowboy. Big in the shoulder, lantern jaw, and a need for silence. Not the kid.

Sam shook himself loose and wondered if he drank

the toothache drops would his head quit rocking and clanging, or would it fall off?

"Kid," he said, "Okay—I'm here. Don't worry."

"We got to ride out of here, Sam," the kid whispered. "Don't talk. Don't make any noise. Just set your saddle."

He felt the kid lift him, and he got his feet wobbling underneath him more or less, and then he felt the kid put his left foot in a stirrup and hoist him on up.

Instinctively his right foot found the stirrup, and he was more or less mounted.

The kid leapt to the pinto's saddle and, taking the bay's cheek strap, led him on down the draw concealed on either side by cottonwoods.

Coming to a dry fork, Tony halted and asked in a low voice, "You okay, Sam?"

"I'm con . . . conval . . . convalesce . . . gettin' better."

"He hit you with a rock, Sam."

"Just one?"

"I guess you'll do." Tony smiled. "Let's get back to town."

"Let's get back to Philadelphia," Sam said.

"Not a chance. Don't you know that by now?"

"I'm learnin'," Sam said, feeling the lump on his jaw and the loose teeth with his sore left hand. "Tell me more."

"For example?"

"For example, how come you're draggin' me out of there instead of me draggin' you?"

"It's a long story. I'll tell you on the way back to Blood Cut."

Julius McCrea sat at a back table in the Bucket Saloon with a glass of Spanish brandy, happy to have something gentler than the rough, yellow-stained whiskey they poured at the bar.

Unobtrusively he observed the scene while at the same time his mind was a million miles away, thinking of what sinister force possessed a man to kill women, to abduct them and sell them into slavery, to dream of being an emperor in the middle of the Republic.

What deep and profound influence had put that evil into the bloodstream? What personal childhood horror had warped the mind to where dominance and debasing of womanhood ruled?

He needed to know the essential mind of the guilty before he could confront him with essential justice.

He lighted his pipe and puffed up a cloud of smoke that obscured him in a noxious haze.

Both Rainy Day and Roark Shado were known to have been in El Paso in the past few years, but he could think of no connection between the strangled woman and either one of them. Day was capable of any violent act, but strangling women seemed out of character, even for him, a gunfighter who would shoot a man in the back unless forced to do it face to face.

He'd not found Day to be a woman's man, although he dressed like a western dandy with his black clothes and silver adornments. It was as if he wanted to be known as the Man in Black, a symbol of the underworld, hell, plague, and famine. Death. With his pale, skull-like features, the image was perfectly evil. Day no doubt believed that he represented unleashed power beyond all of society's constraints, a force above the law to be feared as much as Satan himself.

Still, this wasn't the strangler.

Had Rainy Day wanted to kill that lady, he would have beaten her to death with his gun barrel.

A strangler was a secret person, a man who valued silence, a man who was deceptive. Once removed from personal relationships, using men and women as objects to move other objects, never involving himself directly.

Shrewd and sure of himself, he moved among people as a respected person, yet deep inside he was a Napoleon looking to subjugate and humiliate the rest of the world.

Of course, there were hundreds, perhaps thousands, of men who more or less matched the composite picture, but none that he'd ever seen who wore calf-splat boots with tailored gray trousers and a frock coat.

And there the southern gentleman sat, drawing a puff of smoke from a long, thin Spanish cigar, his evasive eyes catching the glints and glosses of everything going on around him while his mind ranged freely . . . to where?

Where? His mind was looking to consolidate his stranglehold on the western trail, and his mind was ranging toward the future, when the northern territory would become a state and he would be the governor. His henchmen, in white silk shirts, would be there with him cutting up the pie.

That man, a seducer of children, a whoremaster for the sacred and profane rich, those fat fellows like gross, inflated toads, with their diamond rings and carriages, taking girls with their big blue eyes and bouncing bodies and reducing them to trash in a few months. Ah . . . that man. That man must face justice. He must face his countrymen. He must face the parents and brothers and friends of all the girls he had led to the charnel house.

Why the calf-splatter boots? No doubt he'd mistaken a gambler or impersonator wearing boots of that color to be a perfect, chivalrous gentleman of the old days. He'd gotten the rest of it correct. The tailor was right, the single stickpin diamond was right, the thin gold watch chain was perfect.

The trimmed mustache and sideburns addressed weekly by the barber André Brown were proper. No, everything except the boots and the wavering eyes made him appear to be of the old southern aristocracy. But neither one would pass, especially wouldn't pass a lady whose father and brothers had been plantation owners and who, with plumes in their hats and their sabers held high, had charged the Union artillery with unwavering eyes.

But what in the kernel of that man's manhood had warped the seedling? What accident of birth had caused the child's spirit to twist away from rightness and decency?

As a corollary to that question there loomed the other: What real justice can truly be meted out to that man?

You could avenge yourself with torture and death, but would you call that true justice?

Justice should be a positive force that rebuilds what has been destroyed, that supplants evil with good, sickness with health, hatred with friendship.

But how could you transform that pimp or any of his wickedness into something good and decent?

Julius shook his head and sipped at the brandy, knowing he would find no solution past apprehending the criminal and delivering him to a court for what would have to be called legal justice, not human justice.

He puffed at his pipe and tried to let his mind go loose and enter the other's.

Roark Shado puffed occasionally at his cheroot and lazily observed the cowboys starting to get likkered up and the girls coming downstairs to peddle their wares.

He was aware of Julius off in the back corner, but he thought he was a fuzzy-minded old rancher who might or might not have enough backers to buy substantial acreage for a working cattle ranch.

The country was too new for ranching. The Bloods and Shoshones were still active despite the ravages of the smallpox, and no rancher could make a profit while they were still untamed.

The fat man must know that, but he was soft in the head.

He'd never been hungry. Never seen his brothers take to bed with their swollen bellies and the stick legs of rickets.

Never had to run like a rabbit on strange ground from a pack of hound dogs.

Never had to make love to a woman to gain a suit of clothes.

No . . .

But there was something else, if he could only remember it. . . . What was that god-awful thing that happened when he was a little kid? Something about Ma . . . Ma and the overseer who always carried a blacksnake whip coiled about his shoulder . . . How was it? All he could remember was Pa meeting them on the road, eyeing her and the overseer up on his horse with a big, heavy Dragoon revolver in one hand and the Whipstock tucked in his waistband, grinning at Pa, and Ma was crying. That's all he could remember, except the fire that night.

Pa had dumped a couple sacks of rock sulfur around the overseer's house and set her all afire. Then he gathered up the family in the wagon and moved on again.

To Roark Shado's thinking, it had been a stroke of genius to set that kind of fire for that kind of man, but his father never showed any pleasure or pride. If anything, he became more morose and bitter against the world, taking the leather trace to the youngsters with more anger than before.

His pa had tried to battle against his oppressors, but he'd never won. Every year they had gone farther and farther downhill until Ma died and Pa drove the boys out with his leather trace. All Shado remembered of that was the insane anger burning so hot inside his pa's head it seemed like he was all afire with flames shooting out of his eyes and mouth, and smoke from his nose and ears, his curly red hair burning like a torch. It was just an impression that still gave him nightmares.

Years later he heard that his father had set fire to a cotton gin and the big plantation house and then jumped into a river that he couldn't swim.

He fought them all the way, best he could, Roark Shado thought, but he didn't use his head. He let himself get tied down in the system with a no-good wife and a dozen kids so he couldn't win. He never learned how to use people. That was the key. You had to make other people work for you and make a buffer between yourself and all the righteous sonsabitches in the world.

First things first. The secret crossing of the river that came out in old man Packard's back lot had to be taken or sealed off. Another crossing of the river would put Blood Cut out of business, and without Blood Cut he couldn't expand.

You can marry that kid, Nan, he thought, or you can kill them all and just take it.

Killing would be clean and quick. All over in five minutes.

But that Nan girl—a cocky kid, thinking she was leading him around by the nose. No girl had ever led him anywhere. Maybe he let them think so, but he'd broken them all and then left them to wonder what had happened all of a sudden. One day you're a bright, witty, capricious girl, then you meet Mr. Shado, the southern gentleman, and next thing you know, you're an old whore.

That Nan girl was no different. She needed that cockiness taken out of her. She needed to be humbled and debased. She needed to learn how to obey a man and please him.

He decided he'd rather break her than kill her.

Better attend to that today.

Once he had Packard's place secure he was on his way to being the next governor, and if Washington, D.C. got involved in Europe and forgot to watch the western expansion, he was in the saddle for his own little country. If he could control the area to the north, he'd border Canada, and once having that, he could make alliances, play both sides of the fence, and whip them all into proper respect.

Montana Territory. Still mostly Indians up there, almost vacant of white men. Why not start a town up there and gather it into Shadoland?

Need to take a look. Soon as Blood Cut was secure he'd take Day and the crew north and stake out a town. Maybe take over one of the vacated forts up on the Yellowstone.

It was just a matter of timing. Catch the ride right and you can have a country that borders Canada and the United States.

He thought wistfully of taking in Nebraska, Kansas, the Nations, and Texas, and stopping all westward progress of the United States, then absorbing everything west to the Pacific.

He didn't think it was possible now, but he could dream that if he'd lived twenty years before gold was discovered in the Sacramento River, he might have done it.

"Out! Out! Out!" his father had screamed with his face burning from within, and he had murmured aloud very softly, "No, Pa, I'm not getting out anymore, I'm getting in."

Julius saw the southern gentleman's lips move and the distant gaze of glazed eyes and knew he was witnessing the naked man, the evil stripped back to its volcanic fire. Somehow he had to find proof. Genuine, incontrovertible evidence. Somehow he had to fetch this man back to Texas to stand trial.

Yet there could be no evidence. The cord that had strangled the lady could not be traced, and he'd been unable to connect this man with anyone acquainted with the lady named Drusilla Waverly.

The only possible way to convict this man in a court of law would be for him to confess to the crime and plead guilty.

Looking at the tall, lean southern gentleman, Julius had to accept the obvious truth: That monster would never confess to anything.

13

Isham Rye strode into the Bucket Saloon, looked around, and, seeing Julius McCrea at the back table, went to join him.

"Seen that tinhorn Shado?"

"He left only a couple minutes ago," Julius said. "What's your hurry?"

"His time is up."

"Have you any evidence I can use against him?"

"He killed a lady name of Drusilla Waverly in El Paso a year and a half ago."

"I know that case," Julius said. "It's one reason I'm here, but there is no evidence leading to him. There were no witnesses."

"Dru wrote me a letter about a southern gentleman that wore odd-colored boots. That's him. Her sister called him Rory. That's him."

"Where's the sister?"

"She killed herself in Abilene less'n a month ago."

"You talked to her?"

"Yes, but she was too far downhill to make much sense."

"That's the trouble. There aren't any witnesses. The man we're looking for keeps himself screened. You can't hang a man because he wears yellow boots."

"Hellsafire, Julius, there's witnesses right here in this saloon. Talk to any of those girls upstairs."

"I'm game." Julius rose to his feet. "At least we may settle the doubts in my own mind."

They climbed the curved stairs to the landing and walked down the hall where Lily, the henna-wigged, hard-faced madam blocked their way.

"Hold it, gents. You don't come up here unless you got an invite."

"We got the money."

"You're too early. The girls are resting. Come back later."

A door down the hall opened, and Lorena looked at Isham expectantly.

"Sorry," she said, "I thought you was somebody else."

"Wait a minute," Isham called, trying to get around broad-shouldered, mannish Lily.

"Leave her alone and get outa here!"

"Ma'am, I'm gonna bend my gun barrel over your bald head if you don't get out of my way!" Isham pushed on by.

"Lady," he spoke into the open doorway.

"What can I do for you?" Lorena stepped forward again.

Isham saw a packed traveling bag by the door.

"You goin' somewhere?" he asked.

"Sure am." Her speech was slurred and her eyes distant. "Goin' to take a vacation in Havana . . . it's warm and nice there."

"Yes'm," Isham said. "It's a far piece, too. You goin' alone?"

"'Course not. I'm goin' with my sweet man."

"Do I happen to know this lucky fellow?"

"No harm in tellin', I guess—we'll be leavin' this place for good."

"Yes'm." Isham prompted her as her speech dropped to a distant whisper.

"You know the southern gent? He takes care of me, and I take care of—"

"Would that be Mr. Roark Shado?"

"Sure. Ain't I lucky?" She swayed and sat back down on the unmade bed. "Sure. Me and Rory goin' on a ocean liner for a second honeymoon."

Isham looked at Julius. "Any doubts?"

"None." Julius shook his head sickly, staring at the empty-faced woman, her head lolling.

Isham heard boots coming up the stairway and turned to face the balcony.

The red-wigged Lily stopped at the entrance of the hall and said to Mason, coming up behind her, "There they are. Think they own the place."

"You boys lookin' for trouble?" Mason stepped forward.

"No, sir." Isham smiled. "We just was lookin' for company."

"Downstairs." Mason showed his extra teeth in a wolfish grin. "They'll be down later."

"Are you the proprietor?" Julius asked like a country bumpkin.

"My boss is a feller name of Rainy Day. You don't want to meet him."

As the pair advanced up the hall Mason pulled back on the balcony and moved to his left, giving them room to go by.

"Who's his boss?" Isham asked as they came abreast.

"He don't have a boss," Mason replied coldly.

"What about the southern gent? Ain't he boss of somethin'?"

"He ain't nothin'," Mason said. "Just gambles, buys and sells, sits around."

"You serious?" Isham asked directly, unsmiling.

"You want to call me a liar, cowboy?" Mason poised, his right hand caressing the butt of his Colt.

"No. Reckon not. But you got a helluva surprise comin'."

"Downstairs. You can talk to Rainy Day. Now git."

"I don't like to be crowded," Isham said, his tone flat and deadly.

"C'mon, son." Julius touched his arm. "He doesn't know any better."

Mason moved back a step from the force of Isham's anger and decided not to push the two strangers. They sounded like Texans that had just rode up the trail and could be touchy as rattlesnakes in August.

"What did he mean, a helluva surprise comin'?"

Isham and Julius returned to their table and ordered a beer. Hardly had it arrived when a small Mexican entered and went up the stairway where Lily met him and directed him down the hall.

"There she goes," Isham said.

"The southern gentleman sends his regrets." Julius nodded. "He promises to follow along as soon as possible. Meanwhile—"

"I will escort you all the way to Havana," Isham finished for him.

"And maybe Rainy Day is the only one who knows he's the boar coon at the top of the tree," Julius said.

In the oak-paneled office above the bank the southern gentleman lighted a cheroot, leaned back in his chair, and put his glossy yellow boots up on the desk.

To one side Rainy Day stood looking through the window down at Main Street, especially the Bucket Saloon directly across the way.

"I thought I better tell you," Rainy said. "André

Brown heard something about another ford of the river. That Yankee kid was talking to the man that killed Virgil."

"That settles it." Shado lowered his feet and leaned forward to take a small velvet-covered box from a pigeonhole. Opening it, he gazed at the diamond ring for a moment and handed it to Day. "Time to get married."

"Married? At a time like this?"

"You'll understand it better as time goes on, Rainy." Shado smiled. "It's time to bring in all the boys from the cattle camps and downriver. Bring them all in to Blood Cut. We'll be making a move on the north."

"There ain't nothing north till you get to Miles City."

"Maybe we ought to change the name to Day City." The saturnine southern gentleman smiled again. "How many men can we muster?"

"Close to twenty."

"Can they fight?"

"That's what they're paid to do," Day said. "They're all blooded veterans."

"We'll move tomorrow."

"If you aren't the darndest!" Rainy Day exclaimed in admiration. "You set around doing nothing, but all the time you're thinking up something big."

Tony Barr helped Sam down from his horse in the livery stable and followed him to the horse trough where he soaked his head and scrubbed the blood off his face.

"You all right now, Sam?" the youth asked.

"I'm afraid I'll live." Sam tried to shut the ringing gong out of his head but failed.

"Maybe you better go over to the hotel and rest a while."

"How come you were there Johnny-on-the-spot?"

"The cowboy didn't tie me properly because he heard you riding up. They meant to steal the herd as soon as Rainy Day brought supplies."

"And I walked right in on the whole ruckus."

"It's a good thing you did. They'd have killed me for my boots."

"I need a drink," Sam said. "Hope I can hold it down."

"Go ahead, Sam," Tony said. "I'll groom the horses and give them some oats."

"Don't run off again, please."

"Where would I go?"

"You'd be fool enough to go out to that Nan's place and kiss her foot."

"Not me. I learned my lesson."

Sam blearily studied the boy's honest features, shook his head, and said, "Please."

"Don't worry about me, Sam. Honest, I'll be okay."

Sam left the boy in the stable with a curry comb in his hand, but as soon as Sam had walked up the street toward the Bucket Saloon the kid hung up the comb, led the pinto into the passageway, mounted, rode out the back door, and headed north at the mile-eating lope the pinto favored.

Tony felt that he had to try one more time to explain to the girl that he could care for her in a way that would be better than the way she was living now. Certainly she wouldn't be cooped up a million miles from nowhere, and in time his father might relent and lend him enough capital to go into the cattle business.

He had discovered enough figures to show that cattlemen were doubling their money every year by taking up the grasslands just vacated by the Indians and the buffalo. In a year or two, investment money from all over the world would be flowing into these great ranges, so the time to act was right now before the choicest valleys and rivers were taken by big corporations from overseas.

If Nan would just listen to him explain quite calmly the plans that he had made and how he intended to fulfill those plans, she'd understand that he was no longer just a greenhorn kid, but someone capable of loving her and caring for her like a princess if that's what she wanted.

Raised up as she had been, she could ride as well as he could, and maybe better, and she understood how to handle cattle from the breeding bulls to the slaughterhouse.

If she wanted to have that kind of an outdoor ranching life, he could give it to her. If she wanted to be the toast of the city of Philadelphia, he could go along and let her try it until she got sick of the silliness and wanted to go back out west.

But first she had to listen to him.

He slowed the pinto as he neared the ranch. No sense in going in there harum scarum, he thought. Better to make it look like you just happened to be riding by and stopped in to say hello.

He noticed the narrow wheel marks of a buggy on the trail as well as the hoof prints of a riding horse alongside the buggy.

He hoped to God it wasn't that Roark Shado.

Yet, hope to God or not, Roark Shado had tied his matched team to the gatepost and escorted Deacon Trotter to the front porch of the Packard house, where Nan met him.

He did it so smoothly, she hardly knew what was happening, although having expected a proposal of marriage from him made it easier.

"Dear Nan," he said, taking her hand and gazing into her eyes, "I'm going to have to leave Blood Cut in a few days on business, and I've taken the liberty of bringing Deacon Trotter with me for one purpose. Will you be my bride?"

Before she could answer he popped out the jewel box and showed her the flashing diamond wedding ring.

"Say yes and make my life completely happy."

"Oh, Rory, yes, yes!" she cried, throwing herself into his waiting arms.

"When I return we'll take a long honeymoon to New Orleans. Would you like that?"

"Of course, Rory. Anything to get out of this place."

They went inside, and Roark Shado said to the old man, "Mr. Packard, it behooves me to ask you for the honor of your daughter's hand."

"What's that?"

"We want to get married, Daddy," she said excitedly.

"Kind of sudden, ain't it?"

"Yes, but I've important business in Miles City, and I'd like very much to have my bride waiting for me when I return."

"Well, you look like you can afford to take care of her."

"Of course, sir, it's an honor and a privilege."

Her father called in his brother and explained they would be the witnesses to the ceremony, and Deacon Trotter was sober enough to marry them in less than two minutes, once they'd all gotten the idea.

When young Tony recognized the buggy he quietly drifted into the trees where he could watch unseen.

A short time later the deacon came from the house, mounted his horse, and rode back toward the town. Tony knew the worst, but he couldn't accept it until he actually saw it.

Patiently he waited until his beloved emerged from

the house in her prettiest dress. Roark Shado carried her suitcase.

"You can bring my trunk in when you come to town," she said to her father with tears of joy in her eyes.

"I'll do that," her father said. "Good-bye, Nan. Good-bye, Mr. Shado."

They shook hands all around. Shado deposited her bag in the back of the buggy and gallantly helped Nan up.

With a crack of the whip the team trotted back down the road toward Blood Cut.

14

Crestfallen, spirit lost in anguish, young Tony let the pinto follow Shado's buggy at a pace more suitable to a funeral.

Nothing made any difference anymore. The pinto knew the way back to town, he thought; let him go easy.

At a smart trot the matched blacks of Shado smoothly drew the buggy away, while on the stuffed horsehide cushion Nan sat close to her new husband and leaned her head against his shoulder.

"Just think" she sighed happily, "we'll be together forever."

"Yes, my dear," he replied, putting his arm around her waist and holding her close.

"Can't we go on our honeymoon today?"

"No, I'm sorry. Like I said, I've important business in Miles City. It should only take a few days."

Her head bounced against the butt of the .36-caliber revolver in its hideout shoulder holster.

"What's that?" She shifted away from it.

"That's my Navy Colt, my dear. I always carry it for protection."

"Always?" she giggled.

"No, my dear, not when I go to bed." He smiled, eyes gleaming as he thought of the lessons he would teach her in the coming night.

What a silly fool she was! She still believed life was a fairy tale. She was so innocent, he thought he could grow to like her as much as he'd liked any woman; but deep down he knew he'd grow bored with her childishness soon enough and move on to greener pastures while she stayed where he told her to stay and did what he told her to do.

Now, for all practical purposes, he controlled the northern crossing of the Blood. He could leave it hidden, turn his back on it, and move into Montana Territory with Day and Patch, and no one the wiser.

He didn't need to own it, only control it, to be the dominant force of the frontier just as he dominated women, and to take his cut first.

He didn't see this course as a mental problem; he saw it as strictly business, where everything had its price and made a profit.

"Why do you wear those yellow boots, sweetheart?" she asked dreamily.

"Because they suit my style. They're the best money can buy."

"But they look so . . . cheap." She giggled. "Like some poor kid's idea of high style."

"You don't like the color?" He felt the anger building up inside, but his voice was still gentle and cultured.

"It's just that they seem vulgar—something peddlers sell to the Negroes." Again she giggled, unthinking, in her dreamy happiness. "We all call them calf-splatter boots."

He gripped the reins and halted the team, aroused and choleric.

Shoving her away from his shoulder, southern manners gone, he snarled, "Keep your big mouth shut, you little bitch."

"Why, Rory—I didn't mean nothing," she protested, her eyes awake, her mind trying to comprehend the meaning of the abrupt change in his manner. "Nobody's perfect—"

"There is nothing wrong with these boots. They are handmade especially for me in New Orleans."

"That explains it." She laughed.

"Explains what?"

"The calf-splat boots." She giggled again, hoping to tease him out of his black mood.

"I told you," he snarled, and, losing control, he backhanded her across the face as hard as he could.

Suddenly he was inside his raging father, his face aflame, his voice wild. "When I say mind, I mean mind! When I say shut up, I mean shut up! When I say squat, I mean for you to squat!"

Again he struck her as she cowered, bewildered by the sudden alteration in the man she'd just married. All because of a silly pair of boots!

As he cracked her across the face again with his open hand, yelling, "By God, I'll break you!" young Tony Barr came around the bend and heard the unmistakable pop of a hand smacking flesh, the vicious snarl of Roark Shado's voice.

Riding up alongside, he yelled, "Stop it!"

Lost in his fiery anger, Shado hardly heard the hoofbeats or the boy's command. He heard only another threat, another overseer, another humiliation, another barn to burn, and without thinking he pulled the hideout gun from its holster and turned on the youth.

Suddenly Shado recognized Tony as the harmless,

unarmed greenhorn and came out of his uncontrollable rage.

"What do you want?"

"I don't want you hurting that girl," Tony said, staring at the small Navy Colt.

"My wife"—Shado couldn't help lording it over the love-smitten youth—"is none of your business."

"We know all about you, Shado. You're finished," Tony blurted out hotly, without thinking. "My friends will send you to jail!"

"What friends?" Shado sneered to provoke Tony all the more.

"Sam Diggs for one, and Isham Rye, and that old man what's-his-name is a marshal gathering evidence1"

Shado kept his face expressionless, but his mind was racing as he comprehended the force of his enemies.

Nan Packard Shado sat paralyzed in confusion, trying to figure where she fit in this chain of events. Should she run while Roark was occupied with Tony? Should she knock the pistol down and give Tony a chance? Should she believe what she was hearing?

The fact was, she wasn't thinking of saving Tony or defending Roark, she was thinking of what course would be best for her own life.

She saw the knuckle of the trigger finger tighten and heard Roark Shado saying, "Thanks a lot, kid."

She saw the sudden awareness, the terror, in Tony's eyes, saw him fall over the pinto's neck and spur him hard as the Colt fired.

As Tony fell over the frightened pinto's neck the .36-caliber 70-grain ball took him in his exposed right shoulder. Hanging on for dear life, Tony rode the panicked horse away while Shado wasted a shot at his back.

"Damn it," Shado cursed, glancing at the cowering girl and trying to marshal his thoughts.

By the time he got back to Blood Cut Patch and Day should have assembled the twenty gunmen he intended to take up into Montana Territory.

With those men he could wipe out those three strange Texans first and still make the campaign to Miles City, but it had to be done quickly before that fat marshal wired for reinforcements.

The kid was hit and losing blood. He might not make it into town at all.

So all he had to do was reach the safety of the Bucket Saloon and send the troops out after the three strangers.

The plan made, he resumed his southern gentleman manner and smiled at Nan.

"Some kids get so lovesick they'll say anything, sweetheart." He smiled and cracked the whip over the team.

The pinto stampeded with its rider slumped over its neck. Tony knew only that he had to find help. His right arm had lost all strength and was bouncing limply against the pony's shoulder as they entered Main Street and headed for the barn.

Coming inside to its accustomed stall, the pony waited, expecting to be fed, and as old Gimpy approached, Tony slowly slid off to the ground.

"Hey, now—what's wrong?" the old man muttered, not wanting to spook the pinto.

Bending over the sprawled, unconscious youth, the liveryman saw the bloodied shoulder, then crabbed his way toward the street while cursing the pain in his twisted leg.

He needn't have hurried, for Sam Diggs had seen the spotted pony come into the street and go into the barn.

They met on the boardwalk.

"He's hurt bad. I was just comin' to get you," Gimpy said.

Sam hurried inside. "Let me look."

As Sam knelt beside the youth the old hostler led the blood-smeared pinto to another stall and, after unsaddling him, poured a bucket of oats in the feed box as a reward for good behavior.

Sam saw that Tony breathed and that the blood had clotted. He could find no exit hole for the bullet and knew it must still be lodged in the shoulder.

"Is there a doc in town?"

"Sure. He's got a setup in the back of the hotel."

Sam put a ten-dollar gold piece in the old man's hand and said, "That's for thinkin' of me first."

"Don't you worry, mister, I know where I stand in this town," the old man said, smiling.

Sam went on the trot back toward the hotel just as Shado's buggy with its two passengers entered Main Street and turned right.

He met Julius and Isham in the lobby and, explaining as he went, found the doctor's office at the end of the hall.

The room smelled of cigar smoke and iodoform. A tall, gaunt man was pouring whiskey into a glass beaker.

"C'mon, Doc, got a kid gunshot."

"First of the day." The doc lifted the beaker and drank it down, shuddered like a dog coming out of water, then reached for his black bag, all in the time it took Sam to draw a deep breath and get his wind back.

Isham and Julius were waiting in the stable when Sam and the doc arrived. After a brief inspection the doc said, "I can't work in the dirt. We have to get him into my office. It'll be easier to go in the back door."

"Kid, can you walk?" Sam asked urgently. "Hear me?"

"That you, Sam?" Tony murmured.

"Can you walk a ways?" Sam asked again.

"I don't know. . . ."

Getting the boy's left arm around his neck, Sam slowly lifted Tony to his feet, and with the others making sure he didn't fall, they made it out into the alley, through the back door of the hotel, and into the doctor's office, where they laid him on a cot against the wall.

"Now," the doc said, lighting the stub of a cigar, "hold him down while I cut that bullet out."

"Doc, don't hurt him overmuch," Sam said strongly.

"It's not that bad," the doc wheezed. "The bullet's close to the skin."

With Sam holding Tony's shoulder immobile, Isham held the youth's legs. The doc brought out a lancet from a jar filled with alcohol and, with one quick cut, sliced open the shoulder and flipped out the flattened lead slug.

It was out before Tony felt it, and by then his yelp was welcome.

They continued to hold him as the doc swabbed out the hole with alcohol, then let him loose as the doc packed the wound with cotton, bandaged it, and fashioned a sling for the right arm.

Through it all Tony babbled on about the buggy, the girl, Nan, the southern gentleman with the calf-splat boots, making little sense, but when the doc finished and went to wash up Sam asked, "Now, what's all this about Roark Shado? Why did he shoot you?"

"Sam, I'm sorry," Tony said contritely. "All three of you. You're right, I'm just a damn fool kid in a grown-up world."

"What's to be sorry about?" Julius asked.

"He was slapping Nan, and I lost my head. I told him you fellows were after him."

"I'm glad it's out," Isham said.

"He married her out at the house"—Tony closed his eyes to hide his tears—"so why was he slapping her?"

"That's the kind of a hairpin he is," Sam muttered. "You tell him Julius was a lawman?"

Tony nodded and gritted his teeth.

"I'm sorry."

"No need feelin' so down in the mouth. Seems to me you did us all a favor just clearin' the air," Isham said. "Now I can kill the son of a bitch first and explain later."

"No, he's mine," Julius said.

"Don't count on it," Sam drawled. "I reckon what with Patch and Rainy Day and the rest of his gunsels in front of him we can't be too particular."

"This isn't your fight, Sam," Isham said.

"I reckon it sure is. That skunk almost ruined what appears to be my life's work." Sam smiled his hound-dog grimace and patted Tony on his left shoulder.

"Why would he marry her?" Julius wondered aloud.

"My guess is he heard about the river crossing that must be a part of the Packard land," Sam said. "You could open it up in no time with a couple of Fresno scrapers and put this town out of business."

Hardly had he spoken when they heard several pairs of boots climbing the hotel stairway to the second floor and their dull thudding as they went down the corridor.

"Somebody comin' to call on us, Julius." Isham smiled.

Suddenly a burst of gunfire roared from the upstairs hall, and they heard doors splintering and more guns going off.

"He doesn't waste much time," Julius murmured quietly.

Again came the sound of boots clomping down the stairs and loud voices.

"Patch," Sam Diggs said.

"And about six others," Isham added.

When the building was quiet again they heard a faint knock at the door.

Drawing his Colt .44, Isham went to the door, stood to one side, and thumbed it open.

Gimpy scurried in and quickly closed the door behind him.

Looking at Sam, he said, "I want to warn you—there's more hardcases comin' into this town than I ever seen in my whole life, and I figure they'll be lookin' for you."

"They work for Shado?" Sam asked.

"Likely, though it's Patch and Rainy Day ramroddin' the crew. They seen your horses in the barn."

15

Roark Shado sat at his usual back table facing Everett Potter, Marshal Bud Stebbins, Patch, Rainy Day, Mason, and Zinc. Beyond, over their shoulders, he could see the rest of the crew standing at the bar.

"First thing, I don't want anybody getting drunk until we hang those three outsiders. After that we're riding north, leaving Everett and Bud here to keep law and order for us. Understood?"

They nodded, and Bud Stebbins replied, "I can handle it. I just don't understand what kind of a bone those three hombres come this far to pick."

"I don't either," Shado lied smoothly, "but it's not important."

"Maybe they're lawmen," Rainy Day said.

"I doubt it," Shado replied irritably. "What difference does it make? They're trying to take our town from us, and we're not going to let 'em."

"For sure." Rainy Day nodded.

"That's more like it. Now where are they?"

"They wasn't in their rooms," Patch said defensively. "They just disappeared into thin air."

"People don't disappear into thin air, Patch. Think!"

"They ain't here in the saloon. They ain't in the livery or the hotel."

"They ain't in jail." Marshal Stebbins smiled.

"And they ain't robbin' the bank," Everett Potter added nervously.

"Maybe they left town," Mason suggested.

"Their horses are in the livery." Patch shook his head.

"All right, Rainy, take the whole crew out to the end of Main Street and start at the wood yard. Go through it an inch at a time, then check the bank along with Everett, then on to McDowell's Furniture, then through the jail, on into André Brown's place, then the livery again. If you haven't found them by then, cross the street and work your way back, starting at the blacksmith shop."

"And suppose we work our way back to here with no luck." Patch said.

"Then they've somehow crossed the river, and we'll have to track them down. Get moving."

Even as Shado was giving his orders another tapping at the door alerted the men inside. Again Isham stood by the door, gun in hand, and opened it.

Old Hundertmarx and André Brown quickly hurried in and closed the door.

"Gimpy sent us. Said you was set to clean house," the merchant said. "We're ready to help. Most everybody in town is."

"Who knows about this?" Sam demanded.

"Nobody except the folks that been wanting a clean town," André Brown said nervously. "I'm not a gunfighter, but I'm with you."

"We're meeting in my store," Hundertmarx said.

"We been talking for several months, but there never was a chance of us winning before."

"What's in it for you?" Isham asked the merchant.

"Those scalawags, they take whatever they want all the time, and that Shado fellow, he's been looking at my little girl."

"There's about twenty of them down at the saloon," André said.

"And they'll be fanning out through town looking for us any minute," Sam Diggs put in. "We've got to move out."

"The Mercantile?" Julius looked around at the group.

"We go," Isham said.

Sam nodded and said to Tony, "Come on. You and Doc better stay close."

Quickly they filed out of the room, went out the back door into the alley, and hurried to the rear of the Mercantile next door.

After the last one was inside, Hundertmarx dropped a timber into the iron cradles to bar the door.

Sam was amazed to see half a dozen men carrying rifles clustered near the front window. He already knew Gimpy and the blacksmith, still wearing his leather apron, and he nodded to the others.

"Here they come!" Hundertmarx whispered, peering out the window at what looked like a small army searching each nook and cranny building by building across the street.

"They even got men looking on the roofs," the blacksmith growled, loading up an enormous Sharps buffalo rifle. "I could get two with one shot."

"Wait a second, men," Julius said. "We'll need some cover. How about rolling some barrels up here and whatever else will stop a bullet?"

The others, anxious to do something to dispel their nervousness, quickly built a barricade across the front of the store.

"Is there a window in the loft?" Sam asked Hundertmarx.

"*Ja,* front and back for the ventilation."

"Fine. Put the best sharpshooters up there."

The blacksmith and the wheelwright with a long, octagon-barreled Winchester climbed the ladder to the loft.

"Don't fire until I give the word," Julius said, taking command. His calmness and clear voice, as well as a fearlessness born of experience, were enough to dispel any doubts they had about fat older men.

Sam looked at him with admiration, and Isham nodded.

"We're goin' to have to kill all that bunch to get at that rotten whoremaster," Isham said bitterly. "Don't forget, he's mine."

There were no passersby. Women and children and pet dogs were locked in their houses as word spread of a possible battle.

"They'll finish that side of the street and then come back this way," Julius said.

"Sooner or later we're goin' to have to go out and fight 'em," Isham said.

"After we cut them down to size," Julius said, and he turned to Hundertmarx. "Have you a stock of black powder?"

"Sure. Powder, fuse. Down in the basement."

"Basement?" Julius rolled his eyes happily. "Where's the basement?"

Quickly old Hundertmarx lifted up a hatch door and led them down a stairway to a room smelling of earth and housewares.

"Does it connect to the hotel or the saloon?" Julius asked urgently.

"No, not exactly. There's a little space under the buildings, that's all."

Isham ran to the wall and climbed up on a crate. "There's room enough for a man to wiggle through."

"What do you think, Isham?" Julius asked. "A keg on each side—"

"That would do the job with some extra." Isham smiled.

Taking a coil of fuse and lifting the wooden keg of powder up to the ledge, he squeezed himself into the narrow crawl space under the Bucket Saloon and pushed the keg ahead of him.

When he thought he was about under the center of the Bucket's floor he carefully took a thin plug out of the keg and pushed the fuse in.

It was dirty work, and he felt confined and claustrophobic in the narrow space. To be caught in that maze of pier blocks and joists would be worse than being an animal caught in a steel trap.

Sweating from the labor, he tried to keep his mind off the boards hindering his movements. He could hear boot heels pounding the boardwalk a few feet away; there he was on his belly without room enough to even roll over.

When he was satisfied the fuse was secure and wouldn't accidentally be pulled out he wormed his way back toward the Mercantile basement using his knees and elbows.

"Now the hotel," Julius said from the stairway, where he could see the activities in the store.

"Might be some innocent people in there," Isham said.

"We don't set off the powder until we have to. By then the innocents will be gone."

"Well, I don't want to get all dusty for nothin'." Isham smiled and flattened himself in the crawl space under the hotel with powder and fuse.

A few tarantulas and black widows I can handle, he thought, but heaven help me if I come face to face with a big old diamondback rattler.

Positioning the keg under the hotel building, once again Isham removed the thin wooden plug and inserted the fuse. His back was rubbing on the floor joists, so tight was the fit, and he had to squirm back with his chin barely above ground.

Dropping back down into the basement, he said to Julius, "She's ready to fire."

"Fine, Isham, just make sure the fuses are out of harm's way and easy to find. We're going to be a tad busy in a minute."

Isham fastened the fuses so that their ends dangled from overhead timbers, then hung a lighted lamp in between them so that they could be seen even in the smoke and confusion of battle.

"They're movin' the girls out of the saloon," the blacksmith called from the loft.

Sam moved up to check, and from the loft window he saw Lily, with her tall wig like a coil of red-dyed manila rope, herd four girls in scanty apparel out on the boardwalk and into a surrey.

Sam wondered about the girl Nan. Shado must've decided to keep her with him.

But no, the hard-faced madam went back into the saloon and returned with the blond-haired girl. Shado was by her side, talking persuasively, no doubt promising he'd come and get her in a few minutes.

Nan didn't want to go, and she didn't want to stay. She was torn between her fear of the sporting girls and fear of her new husband. Her face was puffy from his beating, and her eyes were wild with fear. She wanted to close off her brain and just scream, but who would hear?

The surrey pulled away, and the town of Blood Cut was ready for anything.

"They're comin' this way now!" the blacksmith called, and Julius came to the window and saw the gunmen emerge from the Niobrara Café, riflemen in the rear covering their movements as they checked every possible hideaway.

"They're thorough enough," Julius said. "Probably good soldiers once."

The sash windows were already raised, and the men crouched behind their barricade.

"Sam, we're going to have to take a bunch of 'em on the first salvo," Julius said, looking out the window.

"Good idea." Sam found five men with rifles at the windows and said, "Pick different men and wait for Julius to give the word."

"I want that one with the fancy belt buckle," Gimpy said.

Sam lined his sights on a man coming up the side walkway as the others rested their rifles on the windowsills and chose their targets.

"There they are!" a man yelled from the roof of the furniture store and funeral parlor across the street, and he snapped a quick shot.

"Fire!" Julius yelled, and the sharpshooters curled their fingers and released a thunderous volley that sent five of the unwary hirelings kicking their lives out on the street or crawling for cover, leaving trails of blood.

Isham fired as the riflemen reloaded. His bullet found a man firing from the barred window of the jail.

"Six down." Julius smiled.

"Heck, that means there's only a baker's dozen left," Sam said mournfully.

He knew he'd brought down one of them, but he'd missed killing him by a couple of crucial inches, and he wondered if his eyes were going bad. Suppose he was to go out and have to draw against one of their top guns. Was he too old to win? Was his arm stiffening up with age, his reflexes slowing down, his eyes blurring?

From outside they heard Rainy Day giving commands as the Shado crew regrouped.

Isham saw the broad, empty street and considered what he would do if he wanted to clean out their fortress.

He had a notion of how it could be done.

"I'll be down in the basement if you need me," he said to Julius, and he hurried down the stairs.

Searching through the stored goods, he found a box half full of heavy brass flower urns, round at the bottom and small at the top—items that would be hard to sell in Blood Cut, which was why they were stored in the basement.

Someday, he thought, if Blood Cut ever became a town safe for women and children, these vases might sit on a mantel full of roses. But then again, that day might never come.

Isham took three urns to the stairway where he could see and cut short lengths of fuse that he inserted in the necks of the vases. Then, unplugging a powder keg, he poured each one full of the grainy black powder.

From another box he found cork stoppers that fit in the necks of the urns, and in no time at all he had made three powerful bombs.

Carrying them upstairs, he set them on the counter near where Gimpy held his position.

"You got to see 'em to blow 'em up," Gimpy said skeptically.

"They've got to come at us one way or another," Isham replied.

"We're pinned in here," Charlie, the wheelwright, complained. "All they have to do is set and wait."

"We've got plenty of groceries." Isham smiled. "We can outwait 'em. Besides, they'll be worryin' about a wagon train comin' through, or maybe a troop of cavalry. They can't wait overmuch."

Isham heard a creaking board above him and studied the angled board roof that had been thinly covered with shakes.

"You got that Sharps fifty," he said softly to the blacksmith. "How about blowing that jasper off the roof?"

"But where is he?" The blacksmith shifted his position.

"Take your time," Isham murmured. "Old Blind Dave will be feelin' his way pretty soon."

As he spoke a faint touch of dust fell from the ceiling, and then another a couple feet along, and another, as if a ghostly blind hand was touching its fingertips to the boards.

Isham saw that the puffs of dust made a line, and he pointed at a knot in the next board. Just as a faint puff of dust fell he said, "Dust him."

The blacksmith pulled the trigger, the knot opened into the blue sky, and a man screamed from above, fell, and rolled like a log off the pitched roof, flopping into the alley.

"With that cannon"—Isham grinned—"I figure if you hit him on the sole of his boot, you probably blowed his hat off."

The blacksmith stared at the hole in the roof as if he couldn't believe what had happened.

"I guess that's the last time they'll send anybody up there again," he said proudly.

From downstairs came desultory firing as the men sought out possible targets while at the same time Shado's men took up rifle positions and commenced a barrage into the front of the store.

The glass in the sash windows splintered immediately, showering the men behind their barricade.

A rifle spoke from the roof of the bank, and the

blacksmith fell back with a spurt of blood erupting from his burly arm.

"Watch the sharpshooters, boys," Isham yelled. "Stay down."

Too late came the warning as a man downstairs grew careless and fell back with a heavy slug in his chest.

"Doc!" Julius yelled.

The old doctor looked up from bandaging the blacksmith. "I've only got two hands. Either stay down or get in line."

"I can finish this," Isham said. "See if you can help that man."

The noise of battle died away as both sides kept to their hidden positions. Occasionally a rifle thundered and gray smoke erupted, but it was more a time of testing each other's defenses.

The rifleman atop the bank was secure behind a brick chimney and steadily maintaining a deadly fire into the front of the store until Isham got tired of ducking.

"That jasper makes me nervous as a duck in the desert," he declared, and he took the blacksmith's huge buffalo rifle, laid the barrel on the windowsill, waited until the sharpshooter fired, rose and took a bead on a brick at the base of the chimney, and fired. The brick exploded.

Diving to the floor, he reloaded and waited until the sharpshooter fired again, rose, sighted in the next brick, and blew it to powder.

"This may take a while"—Isham grinned at Sam—"but I'm goin' to show that feller some daylight soon enough."

Rising, he blew away another brick and dropped to reload.

"Peck away, Isham." Sam made his mournful smile. "I'm bettin' you get him before he gets you."

Another brick disappeared, and Isham had a glimpse of the base of the chimney half eroded away.

Another shot came through the window, and Isham lined up another brick and fired. The bullet tore through a rear brick, and the chimney seemed to totter unsteadily. Isham quick-drew his six-gun and fired at the chimney six times. It was long range, too long, but the touch of his bullets was enough to tip the balance and send the broken chimney over.

The sharpshooter howled in pain, lost his rifle, and clawed at the roof as he slipped downward. He found no handholds left and screamed as he fell into the alley.

"He'll be all right," Sam said. "Probably only broke a couple legs."

As if the sniper's scream had been a signal, a wagon loaded with hay appeared at the end of the street. Timbers had been chained down the exposed side to cover the wheels and the gunmen on the other side.

"Tell Julius this is my play," Isham said as he watched the wagon come slowly down the street, propelled by men concealed behind the hay.

"What you figure they aim to do?" Sam asked.

"They'll park that wagon in front of us and use those logs to hide behind, maybe try burnin' us out."

"If it was me, that's what I'd do," Julius said as he came up to the loft.

"Tell the boys not to do nothin' rash. I've got this here wagon under control."

"But what if they set that hay afire and shove the wagon up against the store? In the smoke they can overrun us," Sam said.

"It ain't goin' to happen thataway." Isham took one of his brass urns with the short fuse sticking out. "Anybody got a light?"

Julius struck a phosphor on the sole of his boot and

held the flame to the fuse. As the powder caught, Isham stepped back on his right foot with his hand cocked, then threw the bomb with all his force, pivoting off his left foot.

The bomb catapulted into the street, but the fuse hit the ground first, pinching out the fire.

"Bad luck!" Isham grabbed another brass urn.

Julius calmly lighted the fuse, and again Isham sailed the bomb into the street. This time it landed on its bottom and bounced toward the hay wagon in front of the store.

"Duck, boys!" Sam yelled.

The street erupted into a mass of loose hay and splintered boards. Amid the thunderous explosion were the agonized screams of half a dozen gunsels who were now left exposed in the middle of the street.

"Fire!" Julius yelled, and the townsmen responded, bringing down the stunned and confused snipers.

"We're gettin' to where we're almost even with 'em," Sam said mournfully.

Again the firing slackened as Shado's men regrouped. Rainy Day, in the bank, was raging as he tried to gain an advantage.

"Try the sides," Shado said calmly, sitting at Potter's desk.

"You mean chop out the walls?"

"Keep them worried about their flanks, then we'll hit them in the front."

"Chango, Red, Mata, Spud—two of you go to the hotel and try to break through with axes and bars. Same for the saloon. Soon as you get a hole made, I'll send you some more men."

"How many have we able to fight?" Shado asked as the four left.

"There's twelve left on their feet. Patch is making sure they don't back down."

"Twelve, plus Patch and you and me. Fifteen

against maybe six in there. We'll tear their guts out," Shado said confidently.

The six townsmen inside the store were not all fighting men. Hundertmarx, André Brown, McDowell, Charlie the wheelwright, Doc, and Gimpy could hardly be called a match for the veteran gunfighters attacking them.

Yet Sam was intact, even though he was worried about losing his master touch, and Isham, though powder-grimed and bleeding from assorted cuts from flying glass, was still strong, and big, heavy Julius seemed like he'd just arrived at the ball, so fresh and happy he looked.

These three, Sam sadly thought, could probably exterminate every back-shootin' skunk in El Paso, Laredo, and Fort Worth in one day. In fact, he couldn't think of a time when he had felt safer than he did right then with his friends on either side of him.

Then he heard the thunk of axes and bars attacking the walls.

"They're tryin' to come in the sides!" Isham yelled.

"I think they just want a diversion," Julius said. "Sam, watch the front like a hawk."

"A diversion?" Isham wondered.

"They know we can use the Sharps and keep them out," Julius said. "They don't mean to push too hard."

"Want me to get the Sharps?"

"No, I want them to think they can come through and put in more men," Julius said thoughtfully, planning his next move.

The creak of boards being barred away and the chopping of axes came from the hotel and saloon walls, and suddenly a wedge of steel came through the wall from the saloon.

"They're mighty close," Isham said, his six-guns ready.

"Don't shoot, Isham." Julius stood solid as a rock. "Sam, let me know if there's somethin' goin' on in the street."

"Some waddies skirting around to the Bucket," Sam called.

"That's fine. Stay there and get ready for all hell to break loose."

A jagged hole appeared in the wall, and Julius nodded to Isham. "Light 'em off, son."

Isham ran to the stairway and down into the basement three steps at a time. Uncovering the lamp, he lighted each fuse and watched the sparks spit as the tiny flames raced away.

"Fire in the hole!" Isham yelled.

Upstairs, he found Julius near the front window.

"Everbody down on the floor," Julius yelled. "Take cover!"

Assured that his men were ready, he knelt behind a barrel of flour and prayed the fuses burned clean and straight.

From the hotel wall came a crash as a whole board was ripped away by a long iron bar, exposing them to hostile gunfire.

Then came the heavy thump swallowed up by the thunder of huge explosions on either side.

Dust and the smoke of black powder poured through the building, and there was no sound of men in agony. There was no one left to scream.

Even as splintered boards fell to the ground outside, Julius stood and lifted both pistols. "Ready, boys! Let's go get 'em!"

"Me first!" Isham yelled, but Julius was a step ahead of him as he leapt over the barricade and out the window into the street. Sam was by his side in an instant, and Isham came along yelling, "Wait! Damn it, wait!"

Coming at them through the smoke and dust were

Patch, Zinc, Mason, and Rainy Day, their guns drawn.

Suddenly men were firing and diving aside.

"Where is he?" Isham yelled, trying to get a glimpse of Shado in the cloud of gunsmoke.

A bullet burned his ribs, and he turned to snap a shot at Patch, catching him in the thigh and driving him to one knee. Rising, Patch tried again, but Julius's bullet punched him right between his little pig eyes.

Isham ran down the street toward the bank as Sam came face to face with Rainy Day, who wanted to run from a battle that was already lost but could not so long as that tall, mournful hound dog of a man stood in front of him raising his .44.

Quickly he jerked up his Colt and fired, his ball turning Sam half around. Yet Sam's arm remained steady and his eye clear as he settled the front sight in the notch on the hammer and, seeing the pearl button on the left shirt pocket, set the two sights just under that and squeezed. The pearl button disappeared into fragments that were buried in the gout of blood bursting from Day's exploded heart.

Julius's next shot caught Mason in the mouth and sent his teeth out through a great hole in the back of his head.

Isham bounded up the steps of the bank.

Before bursting foolhardily through the door he suddenly stopped.

What good would it do to run into a bullet fired by a waiting Shado?

Go slow. Kill him. Once and for all, kill him.

Kicking the door open, Isham waited for a gun to speak from inside, but there was none.

"Come in, please," came the soft southern drawl. "I'm unarmed."

Isham had no choice. He hurled himself sidewise through the door with his .44 at the ready.

Sitting at the banker's desk as if expecting a conference, Shado waited, his hands lying flat on the desk top.

"I swear you're a sight for sore eyes," Shado said calmly.

Isham studied the tall, amiable man at the desk and slowly holstered the six-gun.

"Well, Shado, I been lookin' for you."

"I have no reason to avoid meeting you that I know of, sir."

"You've got reasons."

"Believe me, I am only a land promoter. It seems as if I've been caught in a terrible crossfire, but I belong to neither side."

"I want to kill you, Shado. Kill you slow. First I want to skin you after I whittle on you a while, then I mean to salt you down good, and then, while you're still screamin', I want to lay you out on a bed of mesquite coals."

"That is a fate I don't deserve." Shado smiled. "I'm sure you have the wrong man. Care for a cigar?" he asked politely as he put his yellow boots up on the desk and reached under his coat.

The calf-splat boots broke the hypnotic spell that Shado had woven with his soft, mellifluous phrasing.

Isham drew even as Shado's hand emerged from under the coat with his .36-caliber Navy Colt.

He fired first, and a heavier bullet would have knocked Isham down, but the seventy grains of lead only stung the rangy Isham Rye, whose smokepole came up and belched fire.

The heavy lump of lead tore the gun out of Shado's hand. Shado scrambled to his feet, looking for a place to run or hide.

With teeth bared and hell in his eyes Isham sent the next ball tearing through Shado's left knee, flinging him against the wall.

Shado's hands were raised high as he knelt in a puddle of blood.

"Please!"

Isham's next ball tore out the other knee, dropping him to a crouch. Shado's eyes were wide, and he was screaming, "Please! No! No!"

The next ball tore his right shoulder into fragments of bone and gristle.

"Oh! No! No!"

The next shot tore out the left shoulder so that Shado slumped on the floor with both arms flopping loosely.

Against the hopeless scream ululating from Shado's throat Isham fired again, driving the lead through Shado's bowels.

"This one, Shado—this one is for them all!" Isham gritted slowly, and with his sixth shot he blew Shado's neck bones away, leaving the drooping head to die a little slower.

16

A few days after the battle of Blood Cut, as it came to be known, a new life seemed to emerge from the wreckage. Men were piling up what lumber could be salvaged from the hotel and the saloon, and the broad street was busy rebuilding.

A wagon train stopped to talk of the prospects for settling thereabouts.

Those men who were badly wounded were being kept in the furniture and funeral emporium and attended by the doc.

There were no toll takers, nor a sign of Shado's crew ever having existed. The sporting girls had departed on the first stage going east, whether to go home or to another sordid house no one knew.

Nan had made her way home to her father and lay in bed trying to blot the horror out of her mind. Her father never could completely comprehend the enormity of what had happened nor how close his daughter had come to a tragic end.

His brother didn't believe a word of the story, but he wouldn't go into town to find out the truth. He busied himself crawling down his rows of potato plants squashing potato bugs between his thumb and forefinger.

On the seventh day, when most of the clutter had been removed and people were walking jauntily up and down the streets, planning on building more houses and businesses, a park, and a place for a city hall or a county seat, a buggy driven by a burly man in a derby hat accompanied by an older man in a dark suit and a stovepipe hat arrived in Blood Cut.

The buggy was new and the harness polished bright. The matched team of gleaming chestnut Morgans were the best horses anyone had ever seen, and the older man, whose sunken eyes somberly noted every detail of the town, was obviously a man of great wealth.

"Blood Cut?" the driver asked one of three men standing at the hitch rail.

"Yes, sir, this is it," the mournful, hound-doggy-looking man with his arm in a sling answered.

The driver turned to the older man. "This is it, sir."

"Thank you, Bacon. Ask if they know a boy named Anthony Barr."

Bacon turned back to the threesome and repeated the question.

They looked at one another, looked at the older man with the hooded eyes, and laughed.

"Ask them what's so funny, Bacon," the older man said.

"I'm to ask what's so funny," Bacon said.

With that the trio roared even more boisterously, with great guffaws and backslapping.

"Did you hear that?"

" 'Ask them . . .'!"

" 'Thank you, Bacon . . .'!"

"Just as I surmised," the older man said. "Drunken louts. Drive on, Bacon."

"Wait a second, hombre," Isham said. "Can you talk direct, or do you lose your voice when you're addressing your countrymen?"

"Hummmmpf," the older man snorted.

"Out here a man don't talk secondhand," Sam said, as if explaining to a child.

"It's more efficient," Julius said, his eyes glistening with good humor.

"They are suggesting you should speak to them, sir," Bacon said to his boss.

"I suppose I shan't get an answer otherwise." The older man grimaced.

"That's fair, isn't it?" Isham asked.

"Fair? What's fair in this world?" the old man retorted sharply.

"Maybe where you come from they don't have a thing called fairness, but out here they do," Sam pontificated, his smile hidden in his mournful countenance.

"I'm seeking my son, Anthony Barr," the older man said curtly.

"That's some better, old-timer." Julius grinned. "You're learnin' our ways."

"Old-timer?" The older man seemed to shudder with distaste.

"Well, everybody gets old sooner or later," Sam said, as if overjoyed to be alive. "Even in this climate and this peaceful community."

"Very well, I accept your hospitality." The older man stepped out of the buggy and came face to face with the three westerners. "My name is Anthony B. Barr, Senior."

"I'm Julius McCrea," Julius said. "Pleased to meet you, Mr. Barr."

They shook hands.

"I'm Sam Diggs of St. Joseph, Missouri," Sam said sadly, and he shook hands.

"I'm Isham Rye, from California, and I'm honored to make your acquaintance, sir."

"Please"—Anthony Barr smiled ruefully—"please don't tease me anymore. I know I have a tendency to be a stuffed shirt once in a while."

"Once in a while?" Julius asked.

"I guess it could be cured," Isham said.

"Especially if you had a smart young son to keep you on your toes," Sam said.

"Not too many men are that lucky," Julius added.

"You're right, of course." Anthony Barr spread his hands wide. "I've learned something in the past year that they don't teach at Harvard. Are you acquainted with him?"

"That's for sure," Sam Diggs said. "You probably don't know it, but one of your vice president's assistants hired me to find that boy and deliver him back to Philadelphia."

"But you didn't."

"No, I decided I'd be a genuine purebred skunk if I did such a thing. But at least I did find him."

"It's my fault. I shouldn't have delegated my fatherly responsibility to the staff."

"Well, you're either a father or you're somethin' else," Isham said. "Which is it?"

"I'm Tony's father. Is he all right?"

"There, now, is the question we been waitin' for," Sam said.

"That's it, all right," Julius agreed.

"I thought it would never come," Isham added with a grin.

"Please tell me," Anthony Barr said, pleading.

"He's up and about, I reckon," Sam said.

"Smart, too," Isham said.

"Fine young man," Julius said.

"May I speak to him, please?" Anthony B. Barr asked.

"No," Isham said.

"Perhaps he'd rather not," Julius said.

"I'm inclined to think he'd prefer to be alone," Sam said.

"Look, men—Julius, Sam, Isham, I've come a long way. Doesn't that suggest I'm serious?"

"Does that mean you're goin' to tell him or ask him?" Sam asked.

"You can't tie him down," Julius said. "He's long past that."

"I don't want to tie him down," Anthony Barr growled. "Damn it, I want to find out how he is and what he wants to do."

"There now," Sam said approvingly.

"You might be close," Isham said.

"Have you had your breakfast yet, Mr. Barr?" Julius asked.

"No. First I want to see Tony."

"One and the same," Sam said. "I'll even buy."

"Come on, Bacon, we're going to eat."

Bacon climbed down from the buggy with temerity, looking to the older man for approval.

"Yes, yes, come along, Bacon. Out here in the west men are fair and square." Anthony Barr chuckled and tossed his top hat into the back of the buggy.

The five men made their way across the street to the Niobrara Café, and Isham said, opening the door for Anthony Barr, "Age before beauty."

Tony looked up as the door opened and couldn't believe his eyes. His father!

Not only that—his father was beaming with joy!

Not only that, his father was hurrying toward him with his arms extended as if he was going to hug him!

Impossible!

Tony rose, his left arm still in the sling, and let himself be swept into his father's embrace.

"Oh, Tony boy, how glad I am to see you!" his father croaked weakly, tears in his eyes.

"Gosh, Dad, me, too, and I'm sure glad to see Bacon, too."

As the group settled down at the big table Nan Packard and her father came into the café and took the adjoining table.

Tony's father sat beside him, his arm around his son's shoulder, listening to his son speak.

"Gosh, Dad, you didn't have to come all the way from Philadelphia—"

"Do you think I'm such a heartless father?"

"Well . . . I wasn't exactly sure. Sometimes Bacon told me you wanted to find time for us to talk, but it never seemed to happen."

"It's the new railroad. I got so involved, I almost forgot about the things that count."

"You're building a railroad?"

"Oh, yes, it's well started by now. Within a year it will pass through Wyoming, but that's nothing. How are you?"

Nan appeared oblivious to the talk going on, but even though she spoke to her father about the calf the jersey cow had dropped two nights before, she could hardly keep her eyes off young Tony.

"Yes, Daisy's freshened up—"

"Cattle business! Well, why didn't you say so?" Anthony Barr boomed. "A good-sized ranch with good grass and water is the best investment in the whole country. Better than railroads, steamships, or timber mills!"

"I know the perfect place," Tony said.

"It's yours," Anthony Barr agreed instantly.

"No, Dad, nothing doing. It's mine if I earn it. Nothing less."

"Ah, my son." Anthony Barr's voice dropped to a

somber note. "I understand. You're right, of course. Isn't he, Bacon?"

"I'm proud to say yes," Bacon said.

"I could offer you a loan at a reasonable rate of interest," Anthony Barr offered. "Strictly business."

"I think that would be fair," Tony said, and he looked around at his three friends.

"To be repaid in five years," Julius said.

"That's fair," Sam said.

"I'd say so." Isham nodded.

Nan Packard touched her lips with her napkin and managed to drop it near Tony's feet.

Hardly breaking his speech, Tony picked it up and put it in her lap. "Your napkin, Miss Packard."

He turned back to his table. "Say now, look—I know you're all busy, but could you three help me get started? Just for a month or two?"

"I could spare a month," Sam said.

"Why not?" Julius said. "But I would need to have my family join me."

"How many cowgirl daughters do you have, Julius?" Isham grinned.

"Between the ages of twenty-one and fourteen I have seven."

Miss Nan Packard swooned and would have fallen to the floor had her daddy not caught her first.

Jack Curtis was born at Lincoln Center, Kansas. At an early age he came to live in Fresno, California. He served in the U.S. Navy during the Second World War, with duty in the Pacific theater. He began writing short stories after the war for the magazine market. Sam Peckinpah, later a film director, had also come from Fresno, and he enlisted Curtis in writing teleplays and story adaptations for *Dick Powell's Zane Grey Theater*. Sometimes Curtis shared credit for these teleplays with Peckinpah; sometimes he did not. Other work in the television industry followed with Curtis writing episodes for *The Rifleman, Have Gun, Will Travel,* Sam Peckinpah's *The Westerner, Rawhide, The Outlaws, Wagon Train, The Big Valley, The Virginian* and *Gunsmoke*. Curtis also contributed teleplays to non-Western series like *Dr. Kildare, Ben Casey* and *Four Star Theater*. He lives on a ranch in Big Sur, California, with his wife, LaVon. In recent years Jack Curtis published numerous books of poetry, wrote *Christmas in Calico* (1996) that was made into a television movie, and numerous Western novels, including *Pepper Tree Rider* (1994) and *No Mercy* (1995).